JEFFREY'S LATEST 13
More Alabama Ghosts

JEFFREY'S LATEST 13

More Alabama Ghosts

COMMEMORATIVE EDITION

Kathryn Tucker Windham

With a New Afterword by
Dilcy Windham Hilley and Ben Windham

THE UNIVERSITY OF ALABAMA PRESS
Tuscaloosa

The University of Alabama Press
Tuscaloosa, Alabama 35487-0380
uapress.ua.edu

Hardcover edition published 2016.
Paperback edition published 2021.
eBook edition published 2016.

Inquiries about reproducing material from this work should be
addressed to the University of Alabama Press.

Typeface: Times New Roman

Photographs by Kathryn Tucker Windham (unless otherwise indicated)
Cover design and book illustrations by John Gilbert

Paperback ISBN: 978-0-8173-6034-4

A previous edition of this book has been cataloged by the Library of Congress.
ISBN: 978-0-8173-1912-0 (cloth)
E-ISBN: 978-0-8173-8981-9

Contents

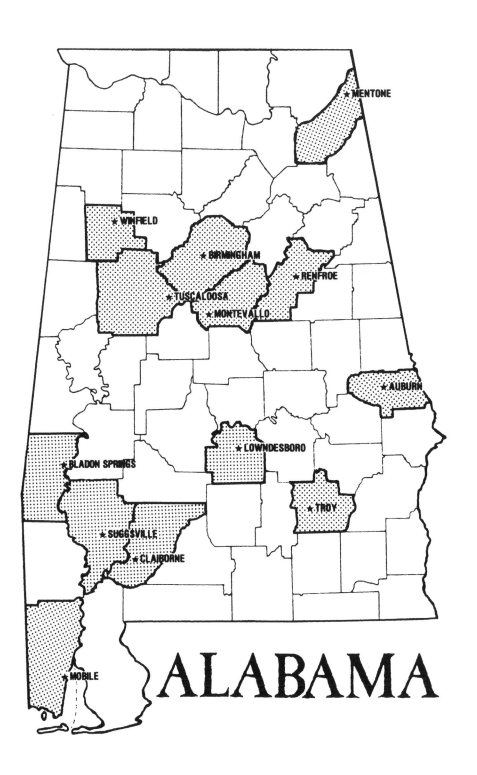

★ MENTONE

★ WINFIELD

★ BIRMINGHAM

★ RENFROE

★ TUSCALOOSA

★ MONTEVALLO

★ AUBURN

★ LOWNDESBORO

★ BLADON SPRINGS

★ TROY

★ SUGGSVILLE

★ CLAIBORNE

★ MOBILE

ALABAMA

Dedication

For Helen and David Akens who, by encouraging me to preserve regional folklore, have made my "latter years" exciting.

Acknowledgments

Many people helped supply information for the stories in this book. Although several of these tales are a part of Alabama's oral tradition of folklore, handed down by word of mouth by local storytellers, details and historical sidelights supplied by interested persons have added to those stories' authenticity.

Singular gratitude for supplying information about these Alabama accounts of the supernatural are due to Mrs. C. F. Graham, Elizabeth S. Howard, Annie Young, Jim Cox, Mrs. Mary P. Powe, Ruth Cowan Redmond, the Bert Neville collection of steamboat memorabilia, Mrs. W. A. Carraway, the *Fort Payne Times-Journal*, the special collections librarians at the Mobile Public Library, *The Clark County Historical Society Quarterly*, Dr. and Mrs. Walter Brower, the staff at the Birmingham Public Library's Tutwiler Collection, Pat Blalock and her staff at the Selma-Dallas County Public Library, the library staff at the Alabama Department of Archives and History, Trudy Cargile, Roy Summerford, Margie B. Huffman, Ann Pearson, Mrs. Robert E. Smith, Mrs. Emma Wilks Petty, Colonel and Mrs. Jerry Doherty, Eva Mae Barfoot Scott, Duck Hardin, Dr. Rosemary Canfield, employees at the Pike County Courthouse, Joyce LaMont and her staff at the William Stanley Hoole Special Collections Library at the University of Alabama, *The Crimson and White*, Mary Chapman Mathews, Mary Frances Tipton and her staff at The Carmichael Library at the University of Montevallo, Mrs. Golda W. Johnson, the *Clarke County Democrat*, the *South Alabamian*, Louis M. Finlay, Jr., Mrs. Emma Norwood Hinson, Judge Otha Lee Biggs, the *Monroe Journal*, the Alabama Historical Commission, and the scores of Alabamians who guided me to splendid stories by asking, "Have you heard about -----?"

Thank you!

April 1982   *Kathryn Tucker Windham*

The Piano

Dr. William Mudd Jordan was a fascinating man. His portrait, hanging now in the home of his grandson, Dr. Walter Jordan Brower, shows his white hair (neatly parted and combed across his high forehead), straightforward eyes, and firm chin. His black bow tie is tied with a surgeon's precision. Only a quizzical lilt of an eyebrow and a hint of a smile at the corner of his mouth betray the sense of humor, the zest for living, that marked his life.

His pipe is missing from the portrait, and that seems a pity. Friends recall that his pipe was ever present, and when he shifted it from one side of his mouth to the other, the movement signaled the start of one of his famous stories.

Many of his stories were about fishing, for fishing was his favorite sport, and he was so successful that tales of his exploits were only slightly exaggerated.

"I've had a lot of practice fishing," he used to say. "I know how." And he did. He retired from the active practice of surgery somewhat earlier than he had intended to: he became allergic to the soap used in scrubbing and had to leave the familiar operating rooms in Birmingham. So he took up fishing.

Dr. Jordan and Ab Sagere, his employee and friend, raised their own bait in elaborate worm beds around his home at 2772 Hanover Circle. He reportedly had the finest worm beds in all of Alabama. When the two men decided their supply of worms was adequate, they loaded Dr. Jordan's car with supplies and headed for the Gulf Coast. Dr. Jordan drove. Ab, who bore the title of chauffeur, rode in the back seat, an arrangement which pleased Dr. Jordan as much as it puzzled his friends.

"We'll be back as soon as our supply of worms gives out," Dr. Jordan would tell his wife, Augusta Sharpe Jordan, as he waved good-bye. She would smile and wave and blow him a kiss. Looking back at her, standing on the steps and waving to him, Dr. Jordan felt a surge of tenderness and pride: his wife was the loveliest, most beautiful, most gracious woman in Birmingham. Many, many people, less prejudiced than he, agreed with him. Too bad, he thought, she didn't enjoy fishing.

With each fishing expedition, Dr. Jordan's store of tales increased, but, though they laughed over his new stories, it was his telling of the old family tales that his listeners most enjoyed.

Sometimes he would tell stories he had heard from his father, Dr. Mortimer Harvie Jordan, Jr., about the cholera epidemic which invaded Birmingham in the summer of 1873. The elder Dr. Jordan was one of the heroes of these terrible times, joining with other pioneer physicians who worked day after sleepless day to minister to the sick and to try to curb the spread of the fearsome killer.

Will Jordan heard his father tell stories of that epidemic often as

12

a boy (some family members thought those stories shaped young Will's desire to become a doctor), and in later years he read with admiration and interest his father's official account, written at the request of the federal government, of those awful days.

Sometimes his father would laugh and say to Will, "You and the cholera came to Birmingham the same year—1873—and the combination was almost more than this town could endure!" So the cholera epidemic was almost a personal thing to young Will, linked as it was with the year of his birth.

He heard stories, too, of his father's experiences as a Confederate soldier with the Forty-third Alabama Regiment during the War Between the States, stories he recalled years later during the long months he served as a major with the medical corps in France during World War I.

And he listened to accounts of the earliest days of Birmingham, of the exploits of men who founded the city. As he grew older, Will Jordan wished he had listened more intently to the tales his father told, that he had written the anecdotes and the trivia that formed the colorful background of Birmingham's early history.

Many of those stories were told on the wide front porch of the Jordan home on the corner of Twentieth Street and Fourth Avenue, North (later the site of The Tutwiler Hotel and presently the site of First Alabama Bank). Dr. Jordan and his wife, the former Florence Earle Mudd, delighted in having guests in their home, and their warm cordiality made the Jordan home widely known for its hospitality.

It was likely in this big house that Lalla, oldest of Dr. and Mrs. Mortimer H. Jordan's six children, first began her study of music. Both Dr. and Mrs. Jordan appreciated good music, and they were determined that their children should take advantage of whatever cultural opportunities the young industrial city offered. So, as soon as she was old enough, Lalla, who was a year older than Will, began to take piano lessons.

Lalla, her teachers discovered, possessed unusual musical talent, and they urged her to continue her studies. Perhaps it was about this time, when her parents recognized and wished to encourage Lalla's

Dr. William Jordan learned to play only two pieces on this Steinway grand, John Philip Sousa's "Stars and Stripes Forever" and Eubie Blake's "Maple Leaf Rag."

musical gift, that she acquired the massive Steinway and Sons Patent Grand piano. Perhaps it was later, after she had married, that the piano became hers. In any event, she spent long hours at the keyboard of that fine instrument preparing for a career as a concert pianist.

"I like to hear you play, Lall," Will used to tell his sister. "To tell the truth, I'm a little envious of you; I wish I could play the piano."

"You could, Will, if you would practice, even a little bit. You're busy with other things, but you really should learn to play. It would give you a lot of pleasure. Maybe you need a piano of your own. Maybe I'll give you this one when I'm through with it!" Lalla laughingly told him.

Lalla did become an accomplished pianist, but she chose marriage and a family rather than devoting her life to music. She never stopped playing though, and her music was a joy not only to her family but also to hundreds of other listeners. If, after her marriage to Ignatious Fenwick Young and after their two daughters were born, she ever wished, however fleetingly, that she had continued her musical career, nobody ever knew about it.

Lalla was only thirty-four years old when she died in 1906.

The piano, the Steinway grand she had loved, went to her brother, Dr. Will Jordan, whom she also loved.

Dr. Will was busy with his practice of medicine, too busy to take time to play the piano. He still wanted to play though, and occasionally he paused by the piano long enough to pick out a tune or two with one finger.

"I'm going to learn to play this piano someday," he promised himself.

Meanwhile, until he had time to carry out that promise, he gave the piano to his daughter, Elizabeth Jordan. Elizabeth had marked musical talent, just as her Aunt Lalla had had, and in addition she had dramatic ability and a beautiful soprano voice. Her talents provided an ideal combination for a career in opera, and that became her goal.

Elizabeth studied under renowned teachers in New York, Italy, and France, and in 1929 she made her operatic debut in Florence, Italy, using the stage name Elizabeth Giordiani.

The Steinway grand was shipped from Birmingham to New York after Elizabeth (she married Walter Scott Brower, a Birmingham attorney) moved there to continue her career as concert pianist and opera singer.

Dr. Will was proud, as any father would be, of his daughter's musical success, but his pride was touched with a bit of sadness. "I just wish Lall could hear Elizabeth play her old Steinway grand. How pleased she would be! Elizabeth is doing what Lall always wanted to do," he used to say. And he'd add, speaking to himself, "Someday I'm going to learn to play—not in public but just for my own pleasure."

And he did. Dr. Will had a good ear for music (the talent seemed to run in the family), and after he stopped being an active surgeon, he had time to practice a bit. His repertoire was limited. He learned to play only two pieces, John Philip Sousa's "Stars and Stripes Forever" and Eubie Blake's "Maple Leaf Rag." It was an odd combination, but it satisfied Dr. Will.

About the time Dr. Will was mastering his two tunes, the Steinway grand came back to Birmingham. It was sent with other furniture to help fill the empty rooms at 3648 Clairmont Avenue when Dr. and Mrs. Walter Brower moved there in 1949.

Dr. Brower, the youngest of Elizabeth and Walter S. Brower's two sons, had moved with his wife and baby son into the old family home while he completed his medical residency at the Jefferson-Hillman Hospital. The Browers' baby was named William Jordan Brower, named for his great-grandfather. Dr. Will was mighty pleased.

Nearly every morning, Dr. Will would go by the Browers' home for a visit with his namesake. Before he left, he would lift the little boy up on the Steinway grand and play for him, first "Maple Leaf Rag" and then "Stars and Stripes Forever." They were still the only pieces he knew.

The little boy delighted in those early morning musicales and would clap his hands and kick his heels in rhythm with his great-grandfather's music.

"You're the only one who appreciates my music," Dr. Will used to tell him. "You don't care if I know only two pieces, do you? Maybe this is how you'll remember me, by my music on this old Steinway grand."

But before little William Jordan Brower was really old enough to remember his great-grandfather, Dr. William Mudd Jordan died. It was 1951, and he was seventy-eight years old. He was buried in the Jordan family plot at Oak Hill Cemetery. William Brower, too young to understand about death, missed his great-grandfather, missed his daily visits and his laughter and his stories and his music.

As the years passed, Dr. and Mrs. Brower kept Dr. Will's memory alive by telling their children (Carl, Caroline, and Frank were born after William's birth) stories about their great-grandfather Jordan. Always they told about his enjoyment of music and of how he played his two pieces on their Steinway grand.

About 1970, when Caroline Brower was in the eighth grade, one of her neighborhood friends, Sally Eastwood, was spending the night with her. The Brower family had moved then to 2832 Balmoral in Mountain Brook, taking the Steinway grand with them. During the night, the two girls were awakened by music being played on the old piano.

"Who's playing the piano?" Sally, startled from her sleep, asked.

Caroline, too frightened to answer, pretended to be asleep. Lying there in the darkness, she pulled the covers over her head and she squeezed her hands over her ears, but she could not shut out the muffled, syncopated rhythm of ragtime. The music continued for a long time. When it finally stopped, Carolina fell into a restless sleep.

As soon as she heard her mother stirring the next morning, Caroline hurried to ask her about the strange serenade.

"So you heard it, too," Mrs. Brower said. "It waked me in the night, and at first I thought I might be dreaming. But I wasn't. That music was a tune your great-grandfather used to play, 'Maple Leaf Rag.'" She hummed a few bars of the melody.

"That's it! That's what I heard last night," Caroline exclaimed. "Who was playing it?"

When Dr. William Jordan died in 1951, he was buried in the family plot at Oak Hill Cemetery.

"I don't know," her mother answered. "Everybody here was in bed. As I said, it's a tune Dr. Will used to play. But surely —" She told again of how Dr. Will used to play the piano on his morning visits and of how eager he was for his great-grandson to remember him. And she wondered.

The eerie midnight concerts continued in the Brower home. There was no pattern or schedule, but occasionally the family would be awakened by an invisible musician playing the Steinway grand, always playing the same two melodies.

In the early 1970s, Dr. and Mrs. Brower and their family moved to Cullman County, to a spacious two-story house built of native stone and timbers. The Steinway grand moved with them.

So did Ab Segere, Dr. Will Jordan's longtime companion. Ab wanted to make sure that the new house was properly protected from evil by having a child's handprint on a wall. He had taken this protective measure in the other houses where the Browers had lived, and he intended to carry on the tradition.

The ghost of Dr. Will Jordan may also have moved to Cullman County. Ab, who was born with a veil, told of seeing the old gentleman sitting at the dining room table eating breakfast morning after morning. Nobody else saw him, but then nobody else in the household was born with a veil.

Other members of the family did hear him though, were awakened by music drifting from the downstairs living area up to the bedrooms that circle the balcony. They lay in bed and listened to the now-familiar program of ragtime and march, and no longer were they frightened. It was almost as if a beloved friend had returned for a surprise visit.

Sometimes, though, those concerts upset overnight guests in the house. The guests, none of them familiar with the story of the phantom pianist, often come down to breakfast and ask, "Who was playing the piano in the middle of the night? I got up and looked over the balcony, but no one was downstairs. But the piano was playing. And it played the strangest combination of tunes, 'Maple Leaf Rag' and 'Stars and Stripes Forever.' Who was it?"

The Browers listen and smile and shake their heads. How can they explain to someone who never knew him that a loving spirit of a doting ancestor lingers in their home? And who would believe that the spirit always plays "Stars and Stripes Forever" and "Maple Leaf Rag," the only tunes Dr. William Mudd Jordan knew?

The Boyington Oak

In 1979, after Hurricane Frederic lashed through Mobile, destroying buildings and uprooting thousands of the city's fine old trees, many people asked, "Did the Boyington Oak survive? Is that old tree still standing?"

The Boyington Oak did withstand the furious winds of Frederic. Its deep, spreading roots held fast, just as they have held against the blasts of scores of other hurricanes since the tree began to grow on the grave of Charles Boyington back in 1835.

That tree, tradition has it, sprang from the young man's grave as proof that he was innocent of the murder of his friend, Nathaniel

21

Frost. As the tale has been handed down, Boyington said to the crowd gathered to watch his hanging, "I'm innocent. I did not commit the murder. And as proof of my innocence, an oak tree with a hundred roots will grown from my grave."

So people watched the mound of earth that marked Boyington's burial place in potter's field, and, strangely enough, a seedling oak began to grow there, began to spread its roots and to flourish. And the people who watched the tree's growth remembered the doomed man's prediction, and they wondered.

Charles Boyington left much to wonder about.

He had no friends when he arrived in Mobile in November of 1833. He came aboard a sailing ship, but no one knows why he chose Mobile as his destination.

It may have been an omen of some kind, an ill-fated omen, that Boyington arrived in Mobile the day after the stars fell on Alabama. Everywhere he went that first day in Mobile, Boyington heard excited accounts of the massive shower of meteors that had illumined the night sky, and he heard muttered predictions, "It's a bad sign."

It didn't seem to be a bad sign for Boyington, not at first. With the help of Captain Arnold, master of the ship that had brought him from New York, Boyington got a job as a printer with the firm of Pollard and Dale. He found pleasant living accommodations at a boardinghouse operated by Mrs. William George, and at that boarding house he found a friend, Nathaniel Frost.

Frost was also a printer, and he, too, was a native of New England. But, unlike robust Boyington, Frost was frail and sickly, suffering from tuberculosis. Boyington appeared to by sympathetic to Frost and even shared a room with him so that he, Boyington, could help Frost at night when seizures of coughing exhausted his puny strength.

On balmy days when Frost felt strong enough (he was able to work only part time), Boyington often took him for walks in the fresh air. They walked slowly and rested often. Frequently they walked out to the city graveyard to read the epitaphs on the grave markers, to admire the work of the stone masons, and to wander among the trees. If

Frost became melancholy and talked of death, Boyington cheered him by reciting a snatch of poetry or by singing a humorous song.

Boyington was an unusually talented young man. Not only did he have a pleasing singing voice, he also wrote almost classical prose, composed stirring poetry, and played the lute, stringed harp, mandolin, and harpsichord well. Those talents combined with his genteel manners and his imposing appearance (though he was only five feet eight or nine inches tall, his erect bearing made him appear taller) won him quick acceptance in Mobile society.

Only a few weeks after his arrival in Mobile, Boyington was invited to attend a holiday ball at the Alabama Hotel, a fine building at the southeast corner of St. Francis and Royal streets. It was at that ball that he fell in love with a young French woman, Rose de Fleur, daughter of Baron de Fleur. Baron de Fleur had been forced to flee France following a duel in which he killed a count who had powerful social and political ties. At least that was the story told in Mobile.

On the night of the ball, Rose de Fleur wore a dress of pure silk, ivory in color, trimmed with scallops and rosettes of handmade blue lace. A late-blooming red rose, cut from the walled garden at her home, was pinned on a cluster of curls in her deep brown hair. As she danced, her dress caught the lights from the hundreds of candles circling the ballroom, and it shimmered in a kaleidoscope of fleeting colors.

Boyington somehow arranged to be her partner for dance after dance until her father frowned his disapproval, and Rose, reared to give strict and immediate obedience to her parents, danced with other young men. Before they parted, Boyington made plans to meet Rose when she went to the cathedral the next morning for early mass. Though Boyington was not Catholic (he professed to no religion), he became a faithful attendant at those early services. He found the ancient ritual beautiful and moving, but, in truth, his attendance was in no way motivated by religion. Rose was there.

Those meetings with Rose at mass (she was always accompanied by a chaperon) provided Boyington a rare opportunity to be with his love. Her parents were very strict, never permitting Rose to be alone, and they discouraged visits from young suitors. So Boyington used trusted servants to slip love notes and poems to Rose, and those same servants notified him when her stern father was away from home.

On those occasions when Baron de Fleur was away, Boyington met Rose for clandestine strolls along Mobile's tree-shaded streets. Sometimes they walked to the city graveyard, a favorite trysting place for lovers, and sat beneath a huge chinquapin tree to talk and to hold hands (always a chaperon followed them at a discreet distance) and to dream of the future. Each time they met, Boyington became more deeply in love with the French beauty.

The days when he could not be with Rose were torture to Boyington. So consumed was he by his love for her that he could think of little else. He lost his appetite (Mrs. George, his landlady, prided herself on setting a fine table, and Boyington's failure to enjoy his food disturbed her), and insomnia plagued his nights.

During many of his sleepless nights, Boyington wrote tender poems of adoration for Rose, and on other nights he struggled to concoct some plan that would make him financially able to seek her hand in marriage. He had arrived in Mobile almost penniless, and his resources had improved only slightly since then.

Boyington's fellow printers, several of whom also boarded with Mrs. George, teased him cruelly about being "love sick." He took their teasing good-naturedly until the day when one of them found a crumpled sheet of paper on which Boyington had written a love poem to Rose. The man waited until just before mealtime, when most of the boarders, including Boyington, had gathered in the big hall to await the ringing of the dinner bell, and then in a taunting voice he read the poem aloud. The hall was filled with laughter.

Boyington was enraged. He lunged toward his tormentor and would have struck him had not two men restrained him. Frost spoke sharply to him, urging him to be calm, and Boyington heeded the advice of his friend.

The mild winter, so different from the bitter cold of the New England winters that both Boyington and Frost had known, drifted into spring. The spring of 1834 was lovely in Mobile. The entire city was ablaze with the fresh beauty of budding trees and flowering shrubs, a beauty so perfect and so fragile it seemed to Boyington to have been created solely as a setting for his beloved Rose.

That spring, as had ten thousand springs before it, seemed to promise happiness to all lovers, but for Boyington that promise was a cruel hoax.

In early April, Boyington lost his job. He had no savings, no resources, and, though he tried, he could find no other work. His situation would have been desperate had not his friend Frost helped him.

"Don't get so upset," Frost told him when Boyington screamed out in hopeless bitterness against his bad fortune. "You'll find a job. And until you do, I'll lend you the money to pay your room and board. The future is not as black as it appears to you right now."

But the spring had lost its beauty for Boyington.

He tried to hide his plight from Rose, but she sensed a change in his behavior and in his outlook. And her sympathy only deepened his humiliation and his despair.

One Saturday (it was May 10, 1834) Boyington returned to the boardinghouse shortly before noon after having spent the morning in an unsuccessful effort to find a job. Frost was leaning against the bannisters on the front porch whittling. The sun felt warm and good on his back. Boyington watched the skillful manipulation of Frost's knife.

"You can carve almost anything, can't you?" he asked.

"No, I'm actually not very good at carving, but I can make simple things. My grandfather taught me what I know. Whittling helps pass the time. It's soothing. Maybe you ought to try it," Frost replied.

Boyington seemed not to hear him. "Could you carve a little wooden heart for me to give to Rose?" he asked.

"Sure," Frost answered. "That will be easy. Maybe we can go to walk after dinner, and I'll work on it then."

So after the midday meal, Frost sharpened his knife and selected a small block of walnut from which to carve a heart. Then the two men set out for a walk.

About midafternoon, Boyington returned to the boardinghouse

alone.

"Where's Frost?" one of the boarders asked. "He didn't get sick, did he?"

"He's all right," Boyington replied. "I just had some things to attend to, so I came on ahead." He hurried to his room.

A few minutes later, he handed Mrs. George a small package and asked that she have it delivered to Rose. Then he left the house.

When the steamship *James Monroe* left Mobile headed for Montgomery that night, Boyington was on board.

The next morning, Sunday, Frost's body was found beneath a chinquapin tree near the Church Street Graveyard. He had died of repeated stab wounds, wounds inflicted by a sharp knife, to the heart.

Monday's Mobile papers carried this official notice from Mayor John Stocking, Jr.:

MURDER—REWARD—Whereas a most atrocious murder was committed within the city of Mobile upon the body of Nathaniel Frost; and whereas, suspicion rests on one Charles Boyington as the perpetrator of the horrid act; therefore, I, John Stocking, Jr., Mayor of the City of Mobile, by virtue of authority in me vested by a special resolution of the Board of Aldermen, do hereby offer a reward of TWO HUNDRED and FIFTY DOLLARS in the event of the said Boyington being convicted of said murder.

The notice of the reward was followed by a description of Boyington and the speculation that the object of the murder was likely robbery. The pockets of the deceased man had been emptied of fifty dollars or more, and his fine gold watch (it had a second hand on its face) was missing, the notice said.

The Thursday (May 15, 1834) edition of the *Mobile Commercial Register and Patriot* carried the announcement that Boyington had been taken into custody aboard the *James Monroe*, was being held prisoner at Claiborne, and would be returned promptly to Mobile.

A sheriff's posse, men who had chased the steamboat with Boyington aboard up river after he fled Mobile, returned the suspect to Mobile on the steamboat *Currier*, arriving Friday, May 16. He was placed immediately in the city jail.

Boyington staunchly maintained his innocence, but a grand jury indicted him for the murder of Nathaniel Frost. His trial was set for November.

During his months in jail awaiting trial, Boyington had several visits from Rose who came to bring him fruit, flowers, and books and to reassure him that she believed him innocent of the horrible crime. Her visits to the jail were stopped abruptly by her father.

Boyington wrote long letters to Rose in which he proclaimed his innocence and pledged his eternal love to her. He also used his time in jail to compose many poems, several of which were published in the local press.

Rose may have believed that Boyington did not commit the murder, but the jury which heard the case found him guilty, and he was sentenced to die on the gallows. Though the evidence against him was purely circumstantial, it was strong enough to convict him.

The execution date was set for February 20, 1835.

Even after the trial, Boyington continued to declare his innocence. His spiritual advisor, Dr. William T. Hamilton, pastor of the Presbyterian Church, urged Boyington to prepare for eternity by speaking the truth of his actions, but Boyington refused to confess to a crime which he swore he did not commit.

He appealed to Governor John Gayle to spare his life, but the governor declined to intervene in the case.

On the day of the scheduled execution, Mobile's streets were filled with people who had come to witness the hanging. They lined the streets from the jail, on St. Emmanuel Street, out to the present Washington Square where the gallows had been built. Whether by accident or design, the route that Boyington's death procession would follow led past the spot where Frost was slain.

It was the custom in those days for the condemned man to ride to his execution seated on his coffin. However, an exception was made in Boyington's case, and he was permitted to walk behind the cart that

Frequently Nathaniel Frost and Charles Boyington walked out to the city graveyard to read the epitaphs.

bore his coffin. Dr. Hamilton walked beside him.

Boyington was dressed in a plain black suit, and he wore a high silk hat which he doffed to friends whom he recognized in the crowds along the streets. He walked in cadence to the music of the brass band leading the procession, and his expression did not change until he first saw the waiting gallows.

He quickly regained his composure, mounted the platform and began to read a lengthy prepared statement setting forth his innocence. When the sheriff ordered a halt to this delaying tactic, Boyington uttered his now-famous prediction about the oak tree that would grow from his grave as proof of his innocence.

The hanging, witnesses recorded, was gruesome, terribly botched by inexperienced hangmen and by a prisoner who struggled for his life.

The event was marked by unusual incidents. As Dr. Hamilton was speaking the last words of comfort to Boyington, Sheriff Toulmin walked over to greet a friend who was sitting on a log near the gallows. Suddenly Sheriff Toulmin fainted. And so did his friend. And at the same instant, the sheriff's horse collapsed in his harness.

Boyington used the confusion resulting from these faintings to make one final effort to free himself from the noose, but his struggle was useless.

The oak, a strong tree with a hundred deep roots, that grew from Boyington's grave, still stands.

After about half an hour, his body was cut down and nailed in his coffin. He was buried (Dr. Hamilton and a few other men who had known him supervised the burial) in the northwest corner of potter's field at the Church Street Graveyard. His grave was near the wall on Bayou Street and only about sixty yards from the place where Frost was slain.

Shortly after he was buried, a tiny oak seedling sprouted out of his grave. Hundreds of people came to look at the seedling and to wonder if it indeed was a sign of Boyington's innocence.

Friends of Frost placed a marker on Boyington's grave, a marker that read:

CHARLES R. S. BOYINGTON

Hanged for the Murder
of

Nathaniel Frost

February 20th, 1835

That marble marker disappeared long ago. No visible sign of the grave remains (the area was cleared for use as a playground years ago and is now used, unofficially, for parking), but the oak, a strong tree with a hundred deep roots, that grew from Boyington's grave, still stands.

Visitors to the spot who listen as bay breezes rustle the leaves of that massive oak hear a repeated refrain: "I'm innocent—innocent—innocent—"

The Silent Riders

It was a sight they never forgot.

As long as they lived, Captain and Mrs. Charles M. Locklin told and retold the story of their predawn encounter with twelve phantom horsemen who cantered out of the McConnico Cemetery near Claiborne back in 1865.

The Locklins were stable, sensible people, not the kind who would concoct a tale about ghosts. Captain Locklin earned his title not as an officer in the War Between the States but as the captain and owner of a steamboat, the *St. Nicholas*.

Having grown up on the high bluff of the Alabama River at Claiborne (Monroe County), Locklin turned naturally to the river for a livelihood. He began his career as a clerk on a packet, worked hard, and eventually owned his own boat.

The Locklin family immigrated from Scotland, settled for awhile in Georgia, and then followed the old Federal Road to the west, stopping in the Mississippi Territory when they arrived at the Alabama River. There was a settlement on the bluff (it stood 180 feet above the water) even then, and John Weatherford, brother of the famed Creek warrior, William Weatherford, operated a ferry there. The site was known as Weatherford's Bluff.

Later, during the War of 1812, United States General F. L. Claiborne built a fort on the overlook and named it Fort Claiborne. After that war, James Dellett, Sr., bought out the Indian claims, and the town of Claiborne was born.

Even then the Locklins were already a part of the town's history. John Locklin had left his Monroe County home to join up with Andrew Jackson's troops as they passed through the area on their way to fight the Battle of New Orleans. He was one of the seven American soldiers killed in that battle.

William Locklin set up a small factory to make Whitney cotton gins in Claiborne, producing his first gin in 1817. He found a ready market for his gins since the river town was the center of a large cotton-producing area.

The Locklin House, also operated by members of the family, was one of the finest hotels on the river, and its food was said to delight all diners.

Being both Scotch and Southern, the Locklins were excellent storytellers, and they found an unending source of material for their tales in Claiborne. Claiborne was the kind of town that breeds stories. Captain Locklin was perhaps the finest storyteller in his family: steamboat captains were expected to tell good tales to entertain their passengers.

Many of his tales centered around the towering bluff at Claiborne. Passengers and crew never tired of watching bales of cotton careen down the long chute from the bluff to the water's edge

Captain and Mrs. Locklin told and retold the story of their predawn encounter with twelve phantom horsemen who cantered out of the McConnico Cemetery.

where roustabouts loaded the bales aboard waiting packets. Sometimes they enticed the muscular laborers to race up the 365 steps (one for each day of the year) with a cash prize going to the winner.

"They built those steps for General Lafayette when he stopped here in 1825, but I don't believe he climbed them. He was too old. I can hardly get up them myself!" Captain Locklin often said.

And then he would tell them stories about the visit of the French general. Or, perhaps, he would tell them the more romantic legend of the Indian princess Winona and her lover, Leopold Lanier.

Lanier, according to the story, was a handsome young militiaman captured by the ruthless Prophet Francis at the Battle of Burnt Corn in July 1813. The prisoner was taken to Nanahubba Island, at the junction of the Alabama and Tombigbee rivers, and tied to a tree to await execution by his captors.

"Then came the romantic part," Captain Locklin would tell his listeners. "Winona, daughter of the Prophet Francis, fell in love with Lanier. She pled with her father to spare Lanier's life, but he replied harshly, 'He will die at dawn!'

"So Winona made her own plan to save the young frontiersman. First she hid a canoe beneath some reeds at the edge of the river. Then, late at night, when all the Indians were asleep, she used a sharp rock to cut the ropes binding Lanier. Stealthily they crept to the river where she showed him the canoe and watched him escape down the dark stream. This done, she crept back to her shelter and pretended to be asleep."

Lanier, Captain Locklin's story continued, loved Winona as deeply as she loved him. They often met secretly in the dense woods near Fort Claiborne, and they made plans to run away, be married, and live a happy life together somewhere near Natchez.

"But, alas," Captain Locklin related, "Prophet Francis learned of their secret meetings. He and a band of his trusted warriors followed Winona one moonlit night when she slipped out of the camp site.

"The two lovers were embracing, standing together on the high bluff, when the warriors suddenly surrounded them. Brave Lanier tried to fight the Indians off, but he was hopelessly outnumbered.

"So rather than endure the torturous death he knew awaited the two of them, he lifted Winona in his arms and leapt into the river," the captain said.

Captain Locklin would then point to the spot from which the leap was made, then show his passengers the approximate place where the lovers entered their watery grave.

"If you believe in ghosts, you might see the ghosts of Winona and Lanier there on the bluff some moonlit night," the storyteller often added with a laugh. Captain Locklin didn't believe in ghosts. Not then.

He became a believer after his eerie encounter with the silent horsemen near the McConnico Cemetery. It happened this way:

Captain Locklin found it necessary to go from Claiborne down to Baldwin County to collect rent on some property he owned there. Money was scarce (it was Reconstruction time, the autumn after the end of the war), but Captain Locklin hoped he could get at least partial payments on the debts owed him. The stacks of Confederate bills in his trunk at Claiborne, enough to make him a wealthy man, were worth nothing, good only as playthings for grandchildren.

The past months had been difficult for them all, especially for his wife, Barbara Moore Locklin. Captain Locklin thought a change of scene, even a trip to nearby Baldwin County, would be good for her. She welcomed the diversion.

Captain Locklin was fortunate enough to own a carriage and good horses. Some of his neighbors had had all their possessions confiscated by the Yankee invaders.

"Those Yankee rascals swept the area clean, took just about everything they wanted without even a 'please' or a 'much obliged,'" he complained to his wife. "Our horses couldn't win a race, but they can get up to Baldwin County and back. And the wheels of our carriage do turn!"

Because they had a long journey to make, Captain and Mrs. Locklin rose long before dawn. While her husband got the horses and carriage ready, Mrs. Locklin cooked breakfast. He ate heartily, but she wasn't hungry. "Journey proud, I guess," she responded when he asked why she was not eating.

She took a wool lap robe out of the blanket chest, and she wondered if she should heat bricks to keep their feet warm. When she asked Captain Locklin, he assured her that the weather was not cold enough for them to need the hot bricks.

"It will get warm when the sun comes up," he said. "Just bring the lap robe, and let's get started. We have a long way to go."

He took his watch out of his pocket to check the time. As always, he handled the timepiece carefully for he prized it greatly. The watch had been given to him by the Mobile Cadets and Washington Light Infantry in 1862 in gratitude for his support of the Confederacy.

"It's later than I thought," he said. "Let's go."

Dawn was an hour or more away, and the moon was shining brightly as the couple set out down the Mt. Pleasant road. There was an autumn chill in the air (Mrs. Locklin was grateful for the warmth of the lap robe), but there was no wind. The only sound was the clopping of the horses' hoofs and the crunch of the wheels on the sandy gravel. The couple was silent, relishing the peaceful beauty of the predawn ride.

Then cantering down the road toward them came two columns of military riders, twelve men on grey horses. The moonlight reflected on the brass buttons on their uniforms and illumined their white-gloved hands. Their hands rested lightly on the pommels of their saddles, and their reins hung loose. As the cavalrymen neared the Locklins' carriage, the columns separated with practiced precision, six riders passing on one side of the vehicle and six on the other.

It was then, as the riders passed their carriage, that the Locklins noticed something very peculiar about them: the riders wore no hats, and each man's head was bound with a white cloth that came across the top of his head and was tied under the chin.

There was something else strange about those riders. Their horses' feet made no sounds on the hard-packed road. There was an unnatural silence as horses and riders disappeared around the curve.

Captain Locklin wanted to turn and watch them out of sight, but his own horses were wild with fear. They snorted and reared and would have dashed headlong into the woods, pulling the careening carriage with them, had not Captain Locklin held fast to the reins.

"Whoa!" he shouted. "Whoa, I say!"

The masterful pull on the reins and the command from the familiar voice quieted the terrified animals, and they slowed to a walk.

Captain and Mrs. Locklin looked at each other and asked almost simultaneously, "Did you see what I saw?"

Each one had seen exactly the same thing: twelve men mounted on grey horses, brass buttons glistening in the moonlight, white-gloved hands crossed on pommels, reins hanging slack, and twelve heads bound with white cloths.

"Did you hear anything?" Mrs. Locklin asked her husband.

"Nothing. Not a sound. Those horses rushed past us without making any noise at all. The silence..."

"That's what frightened me most. The silence. And those white cloths tied around their heads. What was it? What did we see?"

Captain Locklin had no answers, and, though he did not care to admit it, he shared his wife's uneasiness about their strange encounter with the silent riders. They rode without speaking for some time, each one mentally reviewing the details of the scene they had witnessed.

Mrs. Locklin spoke first. "Those cloths," she said. "I keep thinking about them. They're like the cloths used to hold the mouth of a dead person closed, aren't they?"

"Yes," her husband replied. He had helped to prepare bodies for burial and was familiar with the use of the cloths for that purpose.

"But I've been thinking about something else, too," he continued. "Could they have been bandages? Could the cloths have been covering wounds? Could they have bandaged wounds left when ears were slashed off? You don't suppose..."

"You mean those might have been the ghosts of Lafayette Seigler's victims?" Mrs. Locklin interrupted.

"Now I didn't say that. I was just wondering if possibly..."

"I never knew whether to believe those stories about Lafayette Seigler or not," Mrs. Locklin said. "Are they true?"

"Exaggerated perhaps, but basically true," her husband

Captain and Mrs. Locklin
were sure they had met
a group of Yankees
riding out in search of their ears.

answered. "I found them hard to believe, too, at first. Lafayette seems like a nice enough fellow. Hot-headed at times. But I always get along well with him. He hates Yankees though, hates them more violently than anybody I know. It was when I realized how deep his hatred is that I began to believe the stories."

Lafayette (his name honored the French general who visited Claiborne in 1825) Seigler, reliable sources whispered, was so incensed by the lawless actions of Yankee soldiers in and around Claiborne that he began one-man guerrilla attacks upon them.

Seigler had the fastest horse in the county, and his tactic was to entice Yankee horsemen to chase him. This was not difficult to do since they hated Seigler almost as much as he hated them, and each of them wanted the honor of capturing the rebel. The reward offered for Seigler's capture increased their interest in pursuing him.

If one of his Yankee pursuers became separated from his companions, that soldier's horse would likely return to Claiborne without its rider. And Lafayette Seigler would have two new trophies to add to his collection.

It was an unusual collection the young man had. He collected Yankee ears. Some men added notches to their guns to keep count of the enemies they killed. Seigler kept count of his victims by drying their severed ears, folding them neatly, and carrying them in his pocketbook.

Although they had no proof ("How do you prove such things?" Captain Locklin asked again and again), Captain and Mrs. Locklin were sure that they had met a contingent of Lafayette Seigler's victims that predawn morning, had met a group of Yankees riding out of the moss-shrouded city of the dead in search of their ears.

It was a sight they never forgot.

A Promise Kept

Nobody in Suggsville was surprised when Stephen Cleveland took off for California to look for gold. Fact is, most of his friends would have been disappointed if Stephen had not been a part of the 1849 gold rush.

"Just like him," they said. "Let Stephen hear about any excitement going on, and he wants to be a part of it—even if he has to go all the way to California!"

Stephen didn't get in on the first of the California gold fever because news of the discovery of the precious metal at Sutter's Mill was a long time reaching the Clarke County town of Suggsville. It was several months after the discovery that Stephen Cleveland heard stories of the rich gold fields around San Francisco and of the men who were making fortunes there.

As soon as he heard those stories, Stephen was impatient to join the other prospectors heading west. He did not have to ask permission of anybody (he was twenty-two years old, a man grown), so he packed what clothes he figured he would need, tucked what money he had into a wide belt around his waist, and went to tell his family good-bye before he set out to seek his fortunes in California.

His father, James Cleveland, gave Stephen a few parting words of fatherly advice. He knew Stephen was not really listening, but he felt morally obligated to pass along some bits of wisdom to his son. James Cleveland was a staunch Baptist.

So, with his father's advice and with the envious good wishes of his friends, Stephen Cleveland headed west to become a part of a horde of adventurers, many of them young men about his own age, willing to gamble all they owned on the chance of striking it rich in the gold country.

As James Cleveland watched his son ride away, he recalled earlier occasions when he had given unheeded advice to Stephen. For though Stephen had not been an obstreperous child, he was adventurous, headstrong, and reckless. It was Stephen who, though duly warned of the dangers by his father, climbed the tallest trees, rode the wildest horses, and swam the swiftest streams. He had an assortment of scars to show for his exploits, but he had no regrets. "You know I had to try it, Papa," he would say when his father reproved him. "I was scared, so I had to do it. You wouldn't want me to be a coward, would you?"

There was the time when Stephen, about ten years old, planned a reenactment of the Canoe Fight. He, of course, would take the role of Sam Dale, hero of the miniature naval battle. He cast his playmates in the roles of the other participants, though it took a fight or two to persuade some of the boys to play Indians, and he located canoes to use in the drama. The long overland march to the Alabama River was about to begin when James Cleveland learned of Stephen's plans and ordered the group to disband.

"The river is too dangerous to play in," he told them.

Stephen obeyed his father that day. But the following day, while his father was supervising some work on the far side of the plantation, he assembled his cast again and led them to a creek. "Papa didn't say anything about playing in the creek," he assured them as he directed the mock battle betwen the boatload of Indian warriors and the heroes in the canoe.

There were some casualties in the make-believe war, nothing serious, but enough bruises, scrapes, sore heads, and wet and torn clothes to prompt parents to ask questions.

James Cleveland was furious when news of Stephen's escapade reached him. But he forgave him, as he always did, and, later, he even laughed about the episode.

Joining the California gold rush was adventure tailor-made for Stephen.

Weeks and weeks passed with no word from Stephen, but nobody worried about him. He could take care of himself. Always had.

When Stephen got home from California, he looked taller and more muscular than when he had left, and he had a new air of confidence, the look of a man who had run into rough times and had dealt with them courageously. He wasn't cocky, just self-assured.

He didn't bring back saddlebags full of gold nuggets, but he did bring back a store of stories about the places he had been and the people he had met and the experiences he had had.

Stephen also brought back plans for a house.

"I saw a house I liked out there, and I had an architect draw me some plans for one like it," Stephen said. "It's a different kind of house, a good house, and I want one like it. You'll see what it's like when I get it built." He made it plain that he did not want to show his plans or to talk further about his house. When friends asked questions, he replied, "Just wait until I get it built."

It was a rather long wait.

Stephen Cleveland did not built his house until 1860. There were a good many other things he had to do first.

He had entered the practice of law, opening his office in Suggsville, and he had also become involved in politics. He campaigned first for some of his friends when they ran for office, and later he himself ran for the Alabama Senate and was elected to represent the Second Senatorial District (Clarke, Monroe, and Baldwin counties). He resigned from the senate in 1861 to enter military service.

There were family obligations, too. Stephen Cleveland married Eliza Creagh, daughter of his neighbor Gerard Walthall Creagh. On August 6, 1856, their first child, a son they named Walter, was born.

That son, friends said, completely changed Stephen's life.

"Stephen acts as if he's the only papa in the world!" his friends laughed. "To hear him talk, you'd think nobody else ever had a son. Nothing else is as important to him as that baby is."

Stephen was, indeed, a doting father. As soon as Walter could sit up, he took the baby on his horse with him and rode at a canter down the main street of Suggsville. He stopped frequently to introduce his son to friends along the way, to show the baby off. When they returned home, he handed the baby to a nurse and said to Eliza:

"You would have been proud of him—he never cried once! Rode as if he had been born in the saddle. He'll have to have his own pony before long."

Eliza smiled at her husband as she took the baby from the nurse's arms. "Don't hurry with that pony, please. He is a baby yet!"

Walter was still little more than a baby when his sister, Lillian, was born. As soon as he laid eyes on her, Stephen set out to inform everybody he met that Lillian was the most beautiful daughter a man ever had. He believed it, too.

But though he loved her devotedly and catered to her every wish, it was Walter who rode on his horse with him, galloping along the Old Line Road or trotting between the long cotton rows on the plantation; it was Walter who went fishing with him and who "helped" skin the deer he shot; it was Walter who listened to his stories and who learned all the verses of some rather risque songs.

Sometimes Stephen expected too much of his little son. The summer he was almost four, Stephen took Walter to the creek to teach him to swim. The dark brown water frightened the child, and he cried.

"I'm scared, Papa," he sobbed.

"That's all right, Walter," Stephen soothed him. "Don't ever be ashamed of being afraid. You may be afraid, but you are not a coward. There's a difference. Come here and let me hold you in the water."

Before the afternoon was over, Walter was dog-paddling in the creek, no longer afraid. And very proud.

It was that same summer, the summer of 1860, that Eliza and Stephen's house was being completed. Stephen had brought out his plans, had purchased the required materials, and he spent much of the summer supervising the skilled artisans who did the work. The site he chose for the house was on land his wife had inherited at her father's death.

The house was, indeed, unusual. It was a one-story, ell-shaped building only one room deep. Each of the rooms opened onto the front porch and the back porch, giving each room the cross-ventilation so welcome during Southern summers.

The porches were wide with cypress balusters, and the front porch had two sets of steps, one on the north side and one on the east. Those porches were perfect places for children to play.

Once when Stephen had Walter on the horse with him, he urged the horse up the front steps on the east, around the porch, and down the north steps. Walter was delighted ("Do it again! Do it again, please, Papa!" he begged), but Eliza was not pleased. She ran out on the porch and shook her long skirts at them.

"Keep your horse where it belongs!" she shouted at Stephen. She knew he had already ridden out of earshot, but she felt better for having shown her displeasure. Stephen, though he could not hear his wife, knew what she was saying, and he laughed at her display of anger.

Stephen Cleveland was a happy man. He had a fine family, his law practice was flourishing, his agricultural interests were profitable, he had built the house he wanted, and he was a successful politician. Life was good.

Then came The War.

In January 1861, Governor Andrew Moore seized the federal

*Once when Stephen had Walter
on the horse with him,
he urged the horse up the front steps.*

forts and arsenals in the state, including Fort Morgan and Fort Gaines. On January 11, 1861, Stephen Cleveland joined his fellow legislators in Montgomery in passing the Ordinance of Secession.

Walter met him on the porch when he returned from that legislative session. "I missed you, Papa," he said. "Please don't go away again."

Stephen lifted his son and gave him a swift hug.

"You're about to get too big for me to pick up, Walter! You're growing up too fast. I missed you, too." His face became grave. "I wish I could stay here with you and Lillian and Mama, wish I could stay forever, but I have to go away again. The South needs me, and I'll have to go fight. But not right now," he added quickly, seeing the tears about to fill his son's eyes.

"Won't you be scared?" Walter asked.

"Yes, I'll be scared. But I'm not a coward, so I'll go and do my duty for the South."

The next weeks were busy times for Stephen Cleveland. Many business matters had to be settled, legislative affairs required his attention, and arrangements had to be made for the protection of his family before he could volunteer for the new Confederate Army.

It was April, military records show, when Stephen left Suggsville for Fort Morgan on Mobile Bay. He served as captain of a company of Clarke County infantry with the Second Alabama Regiment.

On the day he left for Fort Morgan, the children, worn out from a morning of play, were taking a nap. Eliza started into their room to wake them so that they could tell her their father good-bye, but Stephen stopped her.

"No," he said, "don't get them up. Let them sleep. I am a coward, I suppose—I can't bear to say good-bye to them. You hug them for me and tell them I love them, just as I love you. Remember that always."

And he rode away.

Walter, when he waked from his nap, was hurt and bewildered to find his father gone. "He didn't even tell me good-bye," he sobbed. Lillian was too young to understand, but she cried, too. Nothing his mother said soothed Walter's hurt.

Weeks later, Captain Stephen Cleveland came home on leave. Walter and Lillian, playing with their nurse under the shade of the cedars in the front yard, saw him coming down the drive and ran toward him.

But Walter stopped. He turned away as his father approached.

"What's the matter? Aren't you glad to see me?" Stephen asked.

"You went off without telling me good-bye," Walter replied.

Stephen reached down and pulled the boy close to him. "I'm sorry. I'll never do it again," he promised. "I'll always tell you good-bye."

So when the day arrived that Stephen had to leave to rejoin his company, he called Walter to him.

"I have to go," he told the boy. "You take care of your mama and little sister while I'm gone. I'll be back soon." He started down the steps and then he paused.

"Come on," he said to Walter. "There's time for us to take a quick ride before I go."

Holding the boy in front of him on his horse, Stephen galloped down the road, then turned back to the house and rode up the north steps, around the porch, and down the east steps.

"Do it again! Please do it again!" Walter shouted.

"I will. I'll do it the next time I come home. I promise. We'll have a fine ride around the porch, you and I. Now, good-bye." And Stephen was gone.

But there were no more of those wild, noisy rides around the porch for father and son. Walter died on a July day in 1861. He was almost five years old.

For a while, after the death of his son, Stephen was inconsolable. A grief so heavy that it seemed almost a physical burden pressed down upon him, and there was no escape or surcease.

Perhaps it was an effort to overcome his crushing sorrow that prompted Stephen Cleveland to become involved in organizing a company of cavalry soldiers for the Confederacy. It was easy to recruit members from among his friends in the Suggsville area, but he needed a larger number of horsemen for the outfit.

The September 12, 1861, issue of the *Clarke County Democrat* carried this notice on its editorial page:

"We are requested by Captain Stephen B. Cleveland to state that there is still room for any persons desirous of joining his Cavalry Company.

"All who are not members of the Company may meet in Suggsville on Saturday next for that purpose—and should there be any who cannot get ready by that time, they will still be received by making early application.

There were no more of those wild, noisy rides around the porch for father and son.

"Captain Cleveland deserves great credit for the energy displayed in this truly important enterprise, and with his management and those who are aiding him, there is no doubt of success.

"Every young man now has an opportunity of doing something for his country. We hope all will come forward without delay who intend joining the company."

The next week's issue of the paper carried this news:

"Capt. S. B. Cleveland's Cavalry Company left Suggsville for Mobile on last Monday. It now consists of about 60 men, and as will be seen by a notice in another column, a few more recruits are wanted. This is an elegant company and those who can do so would do well to join it."

Mounted members of the Clarke County Rangers (the unit, sometimes referred to as The Suggsville Gray, later became a part of a regiment recruited by General Wirt Adams of Mississippi) gathered in the yard at the Cleveland home before their departure for Mobile. Captain Cleveland spoke to them briefly, thanking them for their display of patriotism, and then he got on his horse.

Instead of riding directly down the drive to the road, he turned his mount sharply toward the house and rode at a gallop up the north steps, around the porch, and down the east steps.

Some people standing nearby (a large crowd had assembled to bid the company Godspeed) thought they heard him say, "Good-bye, Walter," but nobody was sure. It did seem to be a sort of farewell ritual, a good-bye to a home and to a way of life he loved. And perhaps it was a part of a promise made to a beloved child.

Stephen Cleveland never stopped grieving over the death of his son. It was a grief he carried to his grave, for only at his own death in 1883 was his heart at peace.

The Cleveland house, built with such care, still stands in a wooded area near Suggsville. It is almost unchanged in appearance; even the porches and the steps are the same.

Now a private hunting club uses the house as a lodge. Often, members say, they are awakened around midnight by the clatter of a horse's hoofs mounting the north steps, racing around the porch, and charging down the east steps. There is never a visible horse and rider, just the unmistakable sound of a horse being guided on a familiar route across the porch.

Hunters who hear the sound of the phantom rider say, "Listen. Do you hear that? It's Stephen Cleveland saying good-bye again to his little boy, keeping a promise he made a long, long time ago."

The James T. Staples, *Doomed Steamboat Of The Tombigbee*

Everything seemed to go wrong that January day in 1913. One delay after another forced the postponement of the departure of the steamer *James T. Staples* (usually called the *Big Jim*) from Mobile on her scheduled run up the Tombigbee River.

Aboard the *Big Jim* and all up and down the waterfront there was talk about the recent suicide of Norman T. Staples, designer and former owner of the boat. A pall of sadness over the death of the veteran riverman shrouded the splendid river packet, and the crewmen, men who had once been proud of work on the *Big Jim*, were uneasy, filled with a strange foreboding.

53

They talked in hushed voices about the pride Norman Staples had felt when the boat steamed out of Mobile on her maiden voyage in 1908. His pride, they agreed, was justified: the *James T. Staples* was described as the most elegant vessel then plying the Alabama waters. Some admirers called her a "floating palace."

Norman Staples was a wealthy man at the time he built the *James T. Staples*. Born at Bladon Springs on March 28, 1868, he grew up in the Choctaw County town when it was the center of social and cultural life in southwest Alabama. He drank the waters from the famous springs there; attended the dances, concerts, and parties at the big resort hotel; and hunted in the thick woods near his home.

But it was the river, the twisting Tombigbee, that early claimed his interest. The boat landing was only about three miles from his home, and young Norman delighted in meeting the boats that stopped there. He watched the finely dressed passengers disembark and, with their stacks of luggage, enter waiting carriages to be taken to the Bladon Springs Hotel. He marveled at the strength of the roustabouts as they loaded bales of cotton and unloaded freight, and he learned their rhythmic work songs. He listened as the crews told stories, as they talked of snags, suckholes, sandbars, and currents, and as they discussed news from the various river landings where they had stopped for supplies or fuel.

And on those occasions when he was allowed to go aboard a boat, actually enter the engine room and the cabin and the pilothouse, he knew that his future was forever linked with life on the river.

On still nights, when he was awakened by the deep blast of a steamboat's whistle or when the rollicking beeps of a calliope drifted inland from an excursion boat, Norman imagined himself a pilot or a master aboard a grand steamboat setting out for a lifetime of adventure on the river.

So Norman Staples, when he became old enough, began to work on the river. He was already a pilot, having learned the navigation charts and the uncharted hazards in the state's capricious streams, when his sister, Mary, persuaded him to build a boat of his own. Mary's husband, Fred Blees, was a rich man, and he agreed to finance

The ill-fated James T. Staples
was a sternwheeler
topped by an intricately decorated pilothouse.

the venture.

Staples drew the plans, selected the high-grade lumber used in its construction, and supervised every step of the building of the *Mary S. Blees*. The building was done by James J. Campbell at the Campbell Shipyard in Mobile, and just before Christmas, 1899, the *Mary S. Blees* made her maiden voyage. She was a financial success (it is reported that she made more money than any other boat in the history of Mobile steamboating), and Staples repaid the loan from his sister and brother-in-law in less than two years.

Pleased with the success of his first boat, Staples, during 1905, designed and had James Campbell build for him an unusually wide boat with a very light draught (only sixteen inches when not loaded and only three or four feet when carrying a big load of freight). Some folks said the boat could float on a light dew, but that was a slight exaggeration. He named the vessel for his mother, the *Mary E. Staples*.

Then in 1908, Staples began building the finest boat to be constructed in Mobile since the War Between the States, the luxurious but ill-fated *James T. Staples*, named for his father. The boat was a stern-wheeler topped by an intricately decorated pilothouse. White railings with slender balusters outlined the upper passenger deck, and high up between the twin smokestacks hung a glittering star.

Captain Norman Staples staked his financial future on the success of the *Big Jim*, and his advisors seemed to agree with his prediction that the fine boat would add greatly to his wealth. But 1908, it turned out, was not a good time to invest in a new boat. The Birmingham and Gulf Navigation Company, determined to monopolize river traffic, bought nearly all the boats based in Mobile. A bitter and vicious rate war began between that company and Captain Staples, a financial battle that almost bankrupted Captain Staples.

Competition from railroads became more intense as branch lines spread into the counties along the rivers, causing many shippers to use rails instead of rivers. Captain Staples had failed to foresee it, but the heyday of the riverboat had passed.

It seemed that no matter how carefully he planned or how hard he worked, Captain Staples never had enough money to cover the losses of the *Big Jim*. His debts grew larger and larger. And as his financial condition deteriorated, so did his health. His boyhood dreams of happiness and excitement on the river turned into endless nightmares of disillusionment and frustration and failure.

In late December 1912, Captain Staples' creditors took possession of the *Big Jim*. And, though they may not have realized it, when they took his boat, they also took Captain Norman Staples' hope, his faith in himself and in a better future.

On January 2, 1913, Captain Staples ended his life with a shotgun blast in his chest. He was forty-four years old.

His body was taken to Bladon Springs where he was buried near the graves of his little children: James Alfred, Mabel Claire, Bertha Jaddetta, and one grave marked "Baby." His widow, Dora Dahlberg Staples, and two daughters survived.

The funeral service was attended by hundreds of friends from throughout Alabama, people who admired and respected and grieved for the deceased captain. "Losing the *Big Jim* purely broke his heart," they said. "A part of him will always stay with that boat. As long as she floats, Captain Staples will be around."

Days later, the new owners of the *Big Jim* had difficulty in assembling a crew. Captain William Gray, who had been the chief officer during Captain Staples' ownership, quit in protest of what he considered a "crooked deal" given Staples, and the two pilots, Simon Peter Gray and Ed Jackson, also took other employment on the river. Replacements for the respected rivermen had to be found.

There was trouble with the firemen, too. Men working around the boilers, getting ready for the boat's departure from Mobile, told of seeing a ghost down in the hold of the ship.

"It's Captain Staples," they whispered. "And him hardly in his grave. Ain't no mistake—it's Captain Staples checking things on his boat. His ghost has done come to his *Big Jim*."

And the firemen, one after another, left the boat.

No amount of persuading, no attempts to assure them that they were just imagining things, could lure them back. Each man told the same story of seeing a shadowy figure ("It wasn't no natural man,"

Captain Staples' body was taken to Bladon Springs where he was buried near the graves of his little children.

one of them kept repeating) moving around among the engines and boilers, acting as though he were familiar with each piece of equipment.

"He was just there, Captain Staples was, walking around in his boat, and then the next minute he was gone," one of the firemen reported. "Didn't make no kind of sound. Just disappeared with me looking hard at him. It was a ghost all right. Captain Staples' ghost. I ain't going nowhere on that boat!" Other firemen told almost identical stories.

So the owners had to find new firemen, braver men or men who knew nothing of Captain Staples' suicide and had heard no accounts of his ghost. It was not easy to do.

Finally the *Big Jim* had a full roster of officers and crew, supplies were stocked, freight was loaded, passengers (some of them ill-tempered over the long delay) were boarding, and prompt departure seemed assured.

But then the rats, those big brown rodents that hide aboard boats, began leaving the *Big Jim*. The deck hands saw the first rats scurry across the deck and head for the wharf. Soon there were scores of the varmints stampeding from the boat, fleeing from some unseen terror.

The officers, uneasy themselves, hoped the black crewmen had not seen the rats desert the boat, but they had. And nobody had to tell them what the exodus meant: they knew, as all sailors know, that when rats desert a vessel, disaster lies ahead.

Within a few minutes, the black crewmen also left the boat.

It took half a day to find and sign on replacements.

The officers tried to joke about the jinx that seemed to be plaguing the *Big Jim*, but their laughter was hollow, and their conversation was tinged with uneasy doubts. However, the departure from Mobile, when it finally came, was uneventful, and everything aboard the *Big Jim* appeared to be functioning smoothly. The crew and the passengers relaxed.

On Thursday morning, January 9, the *Big Jim* reached the Coffeeville landing in Clarke County. The boat needed wood to fire its boilers and to warm its passengers (January can be very cold on the

"It's Captain Staples checking things on his boat. His ghost has come to his Big Jim!*"*

river), and there was freight to take on, so the boat tied up.

Gross Scruggs, one of the passengers, took his little daughter, Jennie, ashore to introduce her to some friends. He also wanted to hear what had happened in the area during his absence. "We're nearly home now," he assured Jennie. "Should be there before many more hours pass."

The first mate, W. H. Molton, was also ashore. He had attended to his duties and was about to return to the boat when he saw Prophet, an ageless black man, on the river bank.

"Hey, Prophet," Molton called. "Come over here! I want to ask you something."

Everybody along the river knew Prophet. The old man (he had been old as long as anybody could remember) was a seer, reportedly possessed of a gift that enabled him to foretell the fates of boats on the Tombigbee. The masters and crews of those boats pretended to scoff at Prophet's predictions, but they listened to his slow words intently. And many of those pretended scoffers could cite incident after incident when Prophet's predictions had come true.

"Prophet, what about the *Big Jim*?" Molton asked when the man came near. "Will this be a successful trip?"

Prophet looked out across the river and said nothing.

"Come on. Tell me," Molton said impatiently. "What do you see?"

There was a sadness, a hint of doom, in the old man's voice as he said slowly, "It ain't good, what I see." His eyes were glazed with curtains of cataracts—or was it a film of pending tragedy that covered them?—as he looked straight at Molton. "I don't like to tell you, but you need to know.

"This is the *Big Jim's* last trip. I been seein' her come and go on this river for 'bout five years. But I won't see her no mo'.

"Captain Staples shot hisself. His restless ghost is on the *Big Jim*. And the rats. They left the *Big Jim*. You know that's a bad sign, too. Real bad." Prophet shook his head, looked once more at the boat at the landing, and walked away.

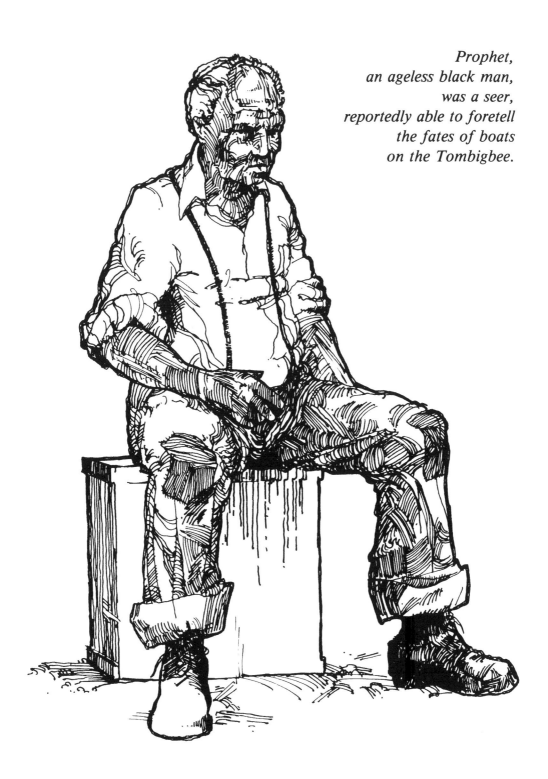

Prophet,
an ageless black man,
was a seer,
reportedly able to foretell
the fates of boats
on the Tombigbee.

"Here!" Molton called after him. "Here's a quarter for you, you doleful rascal!" But Prophet never turned around, just kept on walking.

Molton put the coin back in his pocket. He looked into the faces of the men around him, men who had gathered to hear Prophet's prediction, hoping that they would laugh in disbelief at the words they had heard and that they could all joke together about the crazy old black man. The men stared back at him, unsmiling. Nobody spoke as they boarded the *Big Jim* to continue their journey.

Shortly after noon, the boat tied up at Powe's Landing, about 125 water miles from Mobile, to unload freight. Diners at the first table had finished their midday meal (the *Big Jim* was famous for its food), and the officers were just sitting down to the second table. J. D. Stoudenmire, mate, and two roustabouts were on the landing, making the lines secure and checking the freight. The watch had just changed.

Gross Scruggs, who had eaten at the first table, joined a group of other men on the forward deck for an after-dinner cigar. Jennie waved to her father from the door of the ladies' cabin, and he held up his short cigar to show her that he had only a few puffs left before he joined her.

At that instant, an explosion demolished the front end of the boat. The afternoon calm whirled into a fearful scene of death and destruction. Scalding water sprayed from a shattered boiler, blistering everyone it touched. Screams of the injured mingled with pleas for help as the survivors sought escape from the death trap.

Mate Stoudenmire quickly threw lines to the boat and pulled it to shore. Then he, R. H. Hearin, and others led the women passengers to safety (Jennie Scruggs was carried ashore by Stoudenmire). Once the women (there were five female passengers) were safely ashore, Stoudenmire supervised the rescue of the injured passengers and crew and helped remove the bodies of the dead.

Captain Tom Bartee was killed instantly when his body was hurled into the hold of the boat by the force of the explosion. Also dead were Second Clerk W. C. (Coot) McKee and First Mate Molton. Molton was crushed by a heavy timber, dying before he had time to recall the fateful words Prophet had spoken to him a few hours earlier.

As the last casualties were removed, the *Big Jim* caught fire, burned loose from its moorings, and drifted downstream toward Bladon Springs. It was as though an unseen force tugged at the disabled craft, guiding it down river. When the charred hull finally shuddered and sank, it slid into the muddy waters of the Tombigbee just four miles from the fresh grave of its former owner. The *Big Jim* went down as near to the remains of Captain Staples as a boat could get, as though it were keeping a strange rendezvous.

The explosion and the sinking of the *Big Jim* occurred almost exactly a week to the very hour from the time Captain Norman Staples took his life.

At the time of the tragedy, Captain Billy Simpson, who lived nearby, heard the explosion and came with his launch *Majestic* to aid the victims. He took the passengers and crew up the river to Lenoir's Landing, some four miles away, where the dead were gently shrouded and the living were made as comfortable as possible until the *John Quill*, on her regularly scheduled trip to Mobile from Demopolis, arrived at the scene around midnight.

The survivors were taken aboard the *Quill*, and Captain G. W. Quarles ordered the boat to go full steam ahead to Mobile. A brief stop was made at the Jackson landing to take aboard nurses, family members, and newspaper reporters who had come to that point by special train from Mobile.

Gross Scruggs, as did others, died before the *Quill* reached Mobile. The final tally showed twenty-six persons were killed and twenty-one injured in the explosion.

Although extensive investigations were made, the cause of the explosion was never definitely determined. Various investigators blamed it on faulty boilers (the boilers had been inspected in December and found to be in first-class condition), on dynamite carried as part of the cargo, and on deliberate sabotage. No one ever knew for certain why the *Big Jim* exploded.

*Men working around the boilers
told of seeing a ghost down
in the hold of the ship.*

When news of the sinking reached Coffeeville, Prophet listened to the accounts of the event and to the speculation as to the cause of the explosion. He shook his head sadly and said to no one in particular, "The signs were bad. All bad..." And he walked away muttering about Captain Staples and ghosts and rats.

"I'll Never Leave You"

Many communities in Alabama have local legends about strange images that have appeared on tombstones, mysterious markings with no logical explanations.

There is, for example, the story from Red Level about a man who, many years ago, was riding horseback when his horse ran away, and the man's head got caught in the forks of a low-hanging tree limb. He was killed instantly. The image of a man hanging from a tree limb appeared on the rider's tombstone soon after his grave marker was put in place, the story goes.

Other areas have their own images of devils' heads and black cats and grinning skulls and such that have formed on tombstones. Each of these supposedly supernatural pictures has its own story, a story told and retold, changing gradually with the retellings.

Some of these silhouettes are associated with romantic events, tragic love stories of long ago. One of the best known of this type is the figure of the young girl that appeared on the tombstone of Robert Musgrove over in Fayette County many years ago.

The Musgroves were among the pioneer settlers in northwest Alabama, moving there from the Carolinas with the final wave of emigrants in the 1820s. They brought their household goods and their farming equipment in wagons, jouncing along over the rough roads hewn through the wilderness. They came to stay.

Some members of the family stopped in Walker County while others continued their journey into northern Fayette County where they settled along Luxapallila Creek.

Just as there were differences in opinion among the family as to where to settle, there were sharper differences in loyalties when the War Between the States came along. Many Musgroves served proudly in the Confederate forces while many others remained staunch Unionists. It was a bitter and bloody time with deaths from ambush, torture, hangings, house burnings, and beatings reported frequently (and many not reported at all) in those isolated, wooded hills.

The scars of that conflict had not yet begun to heal when Robert L. Musgrove was born in September 1866. As a boy, he heard stories of death and plunder when armed guerrilla bands enforced their own brands of justice, and he listened to the names of his own kinsmen cast as heroes and villains in those outrages.

As did the other youngsters in his neighborhood, Robert helped his parents with the work on their farm, found time to roam in the woods and along the creek, and attended church at Musgrove Chapel every preaching Sunday.

Members of Robert's family were dedicated Methodists, and, very soon after their arrival in Fayette County, they built a log church which they named Musgrove Chapel. The benches were uncomfortable, and the one-room building was hot in the summer and cold in the wintertime, but the Musgroves filled those rough benches to hear The Word proclaimed, and if their bodies suffered, their souls were revived. Or so they told Robert.

Robert, looking down the benches at the Sabbath gatherings of Musgroves, wondered if his kin had in truth been involved in the atrocities he heard about. He tried to imagine what the men looked like when they were younger.

Musgrove men, old timers recall, were invariably handsome. They, most of them, were tall and muscular, and they moved with the ease and grace peculiar to the outdoorsmen they were. They had ruddy complexions, dark hair, and bluish-grey eyes. It was a pleasing combination.

As he grew older, Robert Musgrove became the handsomest of all the clan. On those rare occasions when he went to town—to Winfield or to Fayette Courthouse or even as far away as Tuscaloosa—it is reported that every woman who saw him walking along the streets stared after him as long as he was in sight and then sighed, "Aaaaahh," softly and longingly.

Robert, they say, never even noticed those stares or heard those sighs. Though he, his friends said, could have had his choice of any beauty in northwest Alabama or northeast Mississippi, Robert wasn't interested in girls. His mind was on trains.

Ever since he saw his first train (there is a difference of opinion over whether this event occurred in Tuscaloosa or in Columbus, Mississippi), Robert Musgrove was obsessed with interest in steam locomotives. He purely fell in love with trains.

"I'm going to be a train engineer," he announced. Trains were all he ever thought about. An engineer was all he ever wanted to be. He wasn't interested in girls at all then, not seriously.

As soon as he was old enough (maybe earlier since birth certificates and child labor laws and such had not been heard of then), Robert got a job on the railroad. He started as water boy for a crew laying tracks, some folks recall, but Robert didn't object to the hard, menial labor. The only thing that mattered to him was that he was working on the railroad.

He was as proud as a man could be when the Georgia Pacific Railway Company opened a line to Fayette in 1883, the first railroad in his home county. Until that time, Tuscaloosa and Columbus, Mississippi, had been the nearest rail terminals to the county seat.

"Now some of my kinfolks can find out how important railroads are," Robert commented. To him, railroads were still the center of his universe.

Robert returned to his family home every now and then, when he had time off from work. If his visits were on Sunday, he always joined his kinfolks and friends for worship services at Musgrove Chapel. After church, when worshippers gathered in clusters to talk a bit before heading home, Robert took pride in telling them about his railroad career.

The St. Louis and San Francisco Railroad was Robert's road, the one he worked for. He had a good boarding place in Memphis, Tennessee, and he was assigned to the run between Memphis and Amory, Mississippi. Robert worked as conductor, brakeman, fireman, and, after a good many years passed, he achieved his lifelong ambition: he became a railroad engineer.

Robert, associates say, treated his engines as though they were living, loving, things, as though the engines understood his respect and affection for them. And the engines responded to Robert Musgrove's attention.

"His engines could do almost anything. They seemed almost to anticipate his expectations, as though they were trained animals instead of masses of metal," they said.

After Robert became an engineer, he relaxed a bit and began diversifying his interests. He discovered, among other things, that girls are nice. And he wished he had made that pleasant discovery earlier: Robert was already well into his thirties then.

For a while, Robert had many girl friends. He was still quite handsome, as all Musgrove men were handsome, and his career as an engineer made him even more attractive to women. So Robert enjoyed his popularity. He had a good time with his female admirers in Memphis, and he delighted in his feminine friends in Amory. There were also a good many young ladies between those two cities whose company Robert Musgrove treasured.

He wasn't quite sure when or how it happened, but a beautiful young woman in Amory captured his heart. It wasn't long before he was thinking of marriage and a home and a family—brand new thoughts for him. Robert had lost none of his enthusiasm for railroading, but love had opened new vistas of joy.

Miracle of miracles, the woman he loved also loved him. When he asked her to become his wife, she accepted. It was spring, the loveliest spring Robert Musgrove had ever known.

He acted like a love-smitten youngster, associates recall, even when he was at work. "Listen to my whistle," he said to his fireman. "Listen. Know what it's saying? It says, 'I'm in love. I'm in love.' I'm going to blow it all the way from Memphis to Amory!" He wanted the whole listening world to know about his happiness.

Then, one dreary night in April 1904, Robert Musgrove was killed in a head-on collision of two trains between Memphis and Amory.

A man on horseback brought the sad news to his family in northern Fayette County.

Arrangements were made to hold Robert Musgrove's funeral services at Musgrove Chapel, the church where he had worshipped in childhood. His body was sent by train from Memphis to Winfield, the nearest rail point to Musgrove Chapel. This was before the days of automobiles, so a caravan of wagons met the funeral train at Winfield to transport Robert's body and the contingent of his friends who accompanied it out to Musgrove Chapel.

Robert's boyhood friends drove some of those wagons. As they waited at the Winfield station for the train to arrive, they talked about Robert, their memories of their good times together.

"Hard to believe Robert is dead," they said again and again. "But if he had to die, it's good to know he died at the throttle of his train. He would have wanted it that way."

When the train pulled into the station, the friends walked quietly to the baggage car, lifted Robert's coffin out, and placed it in the lead wagon. Then they spoke to Robert's railroad friends who had come to his funeral and made sure that these visitors were comfortably seated in the wagons for the ride into the country.

Among the mourners who came on that train was the young woman to whom Robert had been engaged. She rode to the church in the wagon driven by W. L. Moss.

"She was a beautiful young woman. So sad," he recalled years later. "I'll never forget how she looked all dressed in black."

Other people who met her remember thinking how tragic that she should be forced to wear the doleful black of mourning instead of the joyous white of a wedding dress.

The small chapel was filled to overflowing that afternoon with people who cared about Robert Musgrove and who grieved over his death. The altar area of the chapel was crowded with flowers, formal floral arrangements from the city mixed with fresh blossoms (jonquils, pear blossoms, yellow forsythia, and such) cut from Fayette County yards.

The preacher used the Methodist ritual for the burial of the dead, and he read the Twenty-Third Psalm and John Fourteen, "Let not your hearts be troubled..." and he talked about how life is like a railroad. The choir sang "In the Sweet By and By" and "When They Ring the Golden Bells."

Then all the people went out into the graveyard with the preacher leading the way and the pallbearers walking slowly and solemnly behind him.

After the pallbearers had lowered the coffin into the grave and the preacher had said the final words and the grave had been filled, most of the people left the graveyard and started home. They grieved about Robert, but there were chores to do.

The scattering of folks who loitered after the burial saw Robert's sweetheart kneel beside the fresh grave. She folded her hands and bowed her head, and she remained motionless in that attitude of prayer for several minutes. As she arose, people close by heard her whisper, "Robert, I'll never leave you."

Nobody now remembers her name, but nobody who witnessed the sad drama ever forgot how she knelt at the grave or her whispered

promise of eternal love.

Several months after Robert's death, his family had an impressive granite marker erected at his grave, an eight-foot obelisk. Robert would have liked it.

In the years that followed, worshippers at Musgrove Chapel and families who lived nearby noticed that periodically Robert Musgrove's grave was cleared of weeds and fallen twigs, and fresh flowers were on his grave. The flowers were florist's arrangements, not bouquets from local gardens.

"Robert's sweetheart must have been here," the observers commented. And they told again of the events surrounding Robert's funeral, of how his sweetheart whispered, "Robert, I'll never leave you."

Years passed, and the periodic evidences of care for Robert Musgrove's grave continued. Then, as time went by, some woman in the community noticed that there had been no fresh flowers on Robert's grave in a long time. She commented to a friend on the long absence of flowers.

His family had an impressive granite marker, an eight-foot obelisk, erected at Robert's grave.

"Well," the friend replied, "just think how many years it has been since Robert died. His sweetheart must be dead now, too. If she's not dead, she must be too old and feeble to visit the grave. She kept her promise for many years though, didn't she?"

Then one Sunday in 1962 as worshippers were coming out of Musgrove Chapel at the close of the morning service, someone glanced over into the graveyard.

"What's that on Robert Musgrove's tombstone?" she asked. "It looks like a shadow of some kind."

Several people, prodded by curiosity, walked into the cemetery to get a closer look.

There on Robert Musgrove's tombstone they saw the distinct silhouette of a young girl. Her head was bowed and her hands were folded as if in prayer. The silhouette was so distinct that the viewers could see her hair piled high on her head. Even the curve of her eyelashes was quite plain.

"It's Robert Musgrove's sweetheart!" an older man in the group exclaimed. "That's just the way she looked when she knelt on Robert's grave and promised, 'Robert, I'll never leave you.' I was just a boy, but I saw her and heard her—and I'll never forget it."

News of the image of the young girl on Robert Musgrove's grave marker spread quickly throughout that part of Alabama, and curiosity seekers by the hundreds swarmed to the country churchyard.

The invasion of strangers upset members of the Musgrove family, and they tried to remove the image from the stone. But though they scoured and rubbed and scrubbed, the image would not come off. Finally they sent to Birmingham for a stonemason to sandblast the figure from the granite.

With the image gone, the unwelcome visitors stopped coming to the cemetery, and talk in the community turned to other things.

But the image returned, as plain as ever. Again the story of the lover's promise was told, and again the throngs of strangers came to look and to wonder.

The stonemason returned to clean the stone. When he left, the tall marker was as white and unsullied as the day it was put in place.

With the figure gone from the tombstone, the crowds again lost interest in the grave and in its link with the supernatural.

But, they say, the likeness of the grieving sweetheart slowly returned on the surface of the tombstone until, once again, it was as well defined as it had been the day it first appeared.

"She loved Robert very much," the tellers of the story say. "Her love was as strong as her promise, 'Robert, I'll never leave you.'"

There on Robert Musgrove's tombstone they saw the distinct silhouette of a young girl.

The Auburn Spirit

Some years ago down in Clarke County, there was a weekly newspaper editor named George Carleton. He was a wise man, an astute observer of the behavior of human beings and of animals (his stories of wildlife were quoted throughout the South), and he occasionally offered advice to young newspaper reporters.

"Don't ever run the risk of spoiling a good story by investigating it too closely," he used to tell them.

Perhaps George Carleton's advice should have been followed in the matter of the ghost in the old Auburn theatre. Or the ghost who was supposed to haunt that building—some investigators, destroyers of the legend, say there never was a ghost in the theatre.

But it is a good story, a believable story, a story that could be true.

The story centers around University Chapel, the oldest public building in Auburn, and a Confederate ghost who, some tellers say, was named Sydney Grimlett.

Sydney, if indeed that is his name and if the activities attributed to him are true, chose an excellent building to haunt, a building that almost required a ghost!

Construction on the structure, on the corner of College and Thach streets, began in late 1850, and it was completed in September 1851, when members of the Presbyterian congregation held their first services in their new church.

Work on the building was done under the supervision of Edwin Reese, spiritual leader of the Presbyterian congregation in Auburn. It was Edwin Reese who encouraged the town of Auburn to donate a proper lot for the church, who supplied the thousands of slave-made brick (all fashioned on his plantation) used in its construction, and whose family guided the growth of the church for half a century.

The town itself was young when Reese and his fellow Presbyterians built the church. In 1836, soon after the United States obtained the land from the Indians, Judge John H. Harper led a group of Georgians who founded a settlement there.

Judge Harper's son, Tom, mentioned to Miss Lizzie Taylor (she was his sweetheart) that the town had no name. Miss Taylor, who had recently read the poems of Oliver Goldsmith, immediately exclaimed,

"Name it Auburn! 'Sweet Auburn, loveliest village of the plain.'"

So Auburn it became.

Nobody had heard of "War Eagle" then.

But back to the church. By the time the congregation was ready to celebrate the tenth anniversary of its building, Alabama was involved in the War Between the States. Auburn's involvement came early.

Jefferson Davis of Mississippi, soon to be president of the Confederate States of America, reviewed the Auburn Guards as his train passed through the Loveliest Village on February 17, 1861, on his way to Montgomery for his inauguration.

And a few months later, most of the young men at Auburn's East Alabama Male Institute, a Methodist school, left their studies to become fighters for the Confederate cause. The institute, as did many other Southern schools, suspended operation until the war had ended.

Though the students left, the school's main building did not long remain vacant. It was converted into a hospital for the care of Confederate sick and wounded.

And, later, so was the Presbyterian church.

Here begins the actual story of the haunting of that building. In the latter months of the war, a young Englishman named Sydney Grimlett was brought by wagon ambulance to Auburn for treatment of his wounds.

Sydney, they say, was an adventurer, a courageous, perhaps even foolhardy, fellow who relished flirting with danger. Though he was never a bully, Sydney liked a good fight, and even as a boy he had a reputation for taking on any challenger, no matter how big that challenger might be.

Sydney, beneath his toughness, had a compassion for the underdog, and some of his most valiant fights were in defense of someone— or something—who needed help.

He was a strong leader, and early on he learned to use this trait to organize groups of his peers to do his bidding. Some observers called Sydney a soldier of fortune. Perhaps he was.

When the War Between the States began, Sydney read all the articles he could find about the issues involved in the conflict. He talked to such Americans as he came in contact with, principally sailors on ships that docked at British ports, and he questioned them about the progress of the conflict.

As was true with many other Englishmen, Sydney found himself sympathizing with the Confederate cause. And, pretty soon, he decided the Confederacy needed his help.

Sydney boarded a trim blockade runner at Liverpool and sailed off to seek high adventure as a Confederate soldier.

After the ship docked at a Southern port, Sydney made his way to

Virginia where he bought a horse and volunteered for service with the Sixth Virginia Cavalry. At least that's how the story goes.

Before long, Sydney was promoted to captain. The promotion pleased him.

Then in the late summer of 1864, Sydney's unit was assigned to torment, to stage hit and run engagements against, General W. T. Sherman's troops on their devastating march across Georgia. That type of combat suited Sydney perfectly, and the men who served under him boasted of their captain's courage and daring.

It was during one of these guerilla raids that Sydney was struck in the leg by a Minie ball. He managed to stay on his horse until he reached the safety of a Confederate outpost before he collapsed.

The following days were a blur of pain, muffled sounds, confusion, sleep that bordered on death, jostling movement for unending hours, and thirst, searing thirst.

When he roused from the deep blackness that had encased him and when his mind was clear again, Sydney learned that he was in a makeshift hospital in a Presbyterian church in a little town named Auburn.

A surgeon, Dr. L. A. Bryan, examined his wound and dressed it.

"How bad is it?" Sydney asked. "Will I be all right?"

"We'll see," Dr. Bryan answered as he hurried away. He had more than 300 patients to see about, many of them more severely wounded than Sydney.

Sydney lay on his cot and listened to the moans and the screams and the curses of those wounded men, trying to concentrate on their suffering so that he would forget his own pain.

The strategy did not work though. The next time Dr. Bryan saw him (had it been hours? days? weeks?), Sydney was in agony. The doctor removed the bandages, glanced at the leg, and said one word,

"Gangrene."

Sydney knew the rest.

His leg was amputated there in the church at Auburn, a horrible operation, and, though Dr. Bryan and his assistants did the best they could to save him, Sydney Grimlett, captain, Confederate States of

America, died there in that Presbyterian church-turned-hospital.

He had no family, no friends to claim his body, so they buried Sydney in the Pine Hill Cemetery, only a few blocks from the church, buried him along with unknown Confederate soldiers who had also died in Auburn.

For about a century, Sydney lay quietly in his grave. Or so it appears. If his spirit was restless during those years, no account of that restlessness is recorded.

It was not until the 1960s that Sydney's ghost is said to have returned to the site of his death. If it was his first visit in all those years, he must have been startled at the changes. The building he had known

as a hospital had, after the war, been used again as a worship center. Then, after the main building on the campus of the Alabama Polytechnic Institute burned in 1887, the church was used for a time for classrooms.

Later, after the Presbyterian congregation moved into its new sanctuary in 1917, the old church became headquarters for the YMCA.

When Sydney's ghost is said to have appeared, the building housed The Auburn Players, a theatrical group. The Players moved into the old church property in the summer of 1926, and for forty-seven years it was their home.

The actors' move to the former church became necessary when

authorities condemned their quarters, forcing them to leave their "attic theatre" on the fourth floor of Samford Hall. That location in Samford was far from ideal (there was no heat, the stage was cramped, and the clock in the tower interrupted performances each time it boomed out the hour), but during the September 1925-April 1926 season, The Auburn Players staged twenty plays there, a record never since equaled.

They were grateful when Catherine Hare, president of the Y and a member of The Auburn Players, arranged for them to have space in the Y Hut (the old church).

Nobody is sure when Sydney's ghost first made his presence known in the student theatre. Some people say he first returned when The Players were presenting an English play, that he was lured back by the story and the accents from his native land. He was homesick, they say.

After that initial visit, Sydney's ghost practically took up residence in the theatre. In the 1960s and early 1970s (until the new Telfair Boys Peet Theatre was completed), Sydney made his presence known by whistling in the attic, by moving scenery, by a restless tapping of one foot, by producing an eerie overhead light during the production of *Long Day's Journey Into Night*, and by causing props to malfunction.

They knew it was Sydney who did these things, students said, because a Ouija board told them so. After the theatre had been the scene of a series of unusual occurrences, a group of young actors consulted a Ouija board to learn the identity of the perpetrator of those acts.

The board, according to the legend, spelled out Sydney's name and gave them his background.

His presence was so real, so much a part of The Auburn Players, that in the spring of 1971 the award for the most outstanding drama student was named The Sydney Award.

"He never did anything bad," students recall. "He just seemed to want us to know that he was around. He felt at home here," they added. "He was a dramatic person himself, would likely have been a great ac-

Nobody is sure when Sydney's ghost first made his presence known in the student theatre.

tor!''

Not everybody believes the stories about Sydney. Some people say he was created by "street people," protesters left over from the turbulent 1960s, who used the theatre as a sanctuary. It was they, the detractors say, who purely conjured up Sydney.

But there were strange noises and lights in the old building. And stage properties did move. And there were angry foot-tappings. And at least one student, Patty Gerringer, is said to have caught a glimpse of the ghostly image of a man in the shadowy theatre.

If it was not Sydney, could the ghost of the Auburn theatre have been the disapproving spirit of a strait-laced Presbyterian who objected to having such worldly pastimes as theatrical productions presented in a building built for worship?

Whoever it was and whatever his mission, the ghost no longer haunts the building on the corner of Thach and College. In its most recent renovation, it has been rededicated as a place of worship, The University Chapel.

Sydney, it is rumored, is trying to become comfortable in Auburn University's new Peet Theatre.

A Sampling Of
University Hauntings

Colleges, it appears, have always been attractive to ghosts, and there is hardly an institution of higher learning in Alabama that lacks a local legend of the supernatural.

Huntingdon College has its Red Lady, Judson has its phantom organist, Montevallo has the restless spirit of a former student up on fourth Main (better known as Buzzard), Spring Hill has the ghost of a brilliant mathematics professor, Athens College has the stern presence of Madam Childs, and there are other such college hauntings.

The University of Alabama, as befits the state's oldest seat of advanced education, has several college ghosts, spirits linked with the history of that Tuscaloosa institution. Ghost lore on the University campus centers on Smith Hall where for more than a quarter of a century there have been stories of nocturnal noises for which there is no satisfactory explanation.

There may have been earlier supernatural occurrences in the yellow brick building, but it was in 1955 that Dr. Gary Hooks, then an instructor at the University, had his first encounters with the Smith Hall ghosts. Dr. Hooks, it is recorded, was working very late, doing research for his dissertation in a room on the first floor of Smith Hall. He was alone in the building.

He was concentrating on the notes and charts spread out in front of him when he became aware of unusual noises on the floor above him. There were the sounds of muffled voices and of many footsteps, as though a group of students was being shown through the second-floor museum.

Dr. Hooks hurried upstairs to see who the late-night visitors were, but he found the second floor quite deserted: no one was there. There was no one on the third floor, either. Yet Dr. Hooks was certain he had heard footsteps and voices.

He gathered up his papers and left the building.

This initial awareness of the presence of other people in the supposedly empty building was followed by several similar experiences. Again and again his late night study was interrupted by clattering footsteps on the second floor and by the intermingling of many voices. And on each such occasion, a search of the building showed no one else was there.

The ghostly noises did not always follow the same pattern. Sometimes it was the voices of college students Dr. Hooks heard, as though the students were assembling in the classroom for a lecture or were changing classes. At other times the voices seemed to be those of children, perhaps elementary school pupils being taken on a tour of the museum. Though thousands of Alabama schoolchildren have trekked through the museum in the past half-century, no youngsters were ever visible when Dr. Hooks went to investigate.

In the early 1970s, several graduate students studying past midnight in Smith Hall told of eerie experiences similar to those reported by Dr. Hooks.

Chuck Weilchowsky of Selma, working alone in the basement after midnight, had his study interrupted by the same kinds of noises, the subdued intermingling of many voices and the hurried steps of many feet. But never did he find anyone else in the building.

Bob Clark, Barry Gilliam, Jay Masingill, Perry Hubbert, Vic Davis, Steve Kimbrell, and others have reportedly heard the phanton voices and footsteps. On some occasions, they said, a dominant voice was audible above the murmur. Though the words were not clear enough to be understood, it sounded, they said, like the voice of a teacher or lecturer calling his class to order.

Occasionally, these graduate students recalled, they were aware of an unseen presence very close to them, as though a professor were looking over their shoulders to check the quality of their research.

Some of the students who heard the ghostly noises believe the sounds somehow involve Dr. Eugene Allen Smith for whom the building was named.

Dr. Smith was born in Autauga County in 1841, and he entered the University of Alabama in 1860. The War Between the States interrupted his education, and in 1862 he joined the Confederate forces, attaining the rank of captain.

He became a professor on the faculty of the University in 1871, having earlier earned his Ph.D. degree from Heidelburg University. In 1873, the Alabama legislature appointed him Alabama's first state geologist.

In his new position, Dr. Smith crisscrossed the state in his horse-drawn buggy, observing, studying, mapping, collecting, photographing, and writing about Alabama's geological formations. It was Dr. Smith who first recognized the importance of preserving the remnants of Indian culture at Moundville.

He was nearly seventy years old, but still quite active, when Smith Hall was completed in 1910. He moved his laboratory to the first floor of the building that bears his name, and for the next seventeen years he continued to work there. And into that building he brought his collec-

Dr. Eugene Allen Smith spent most of the last years of his long life in Smith Hall.

tion of fossils, artifacts, and rocks, geological samples from every county in the state.

Dr. Smith was eating breakfast one morning in late August 1927, when he became violently ill. His death came about a week later. He was eighty-six years old.

"Dr. Smith spent most of the last years of his long life in Smith Hall. He loved this place," students who believe that his spirit still lingers in the building point out. "He liked to lecture to the classes and enjoyed escorting groups of elementary schoolchildren through the Museum of Natural History, talking to them and answering their questions.

"He dedicated his life to the study of the geology of his native state, and he wanted to pass his knowledge on to new generations. So it could well be his voice we hear above the mingled whispers, his footsteps we hear in the museum, his presence we feel," they say.

It is not so easy to put actual names to the ghosts who haunt the Little Round House, though the circumstances surrounding their reported hauntings are well documented.

According to the story told by generations of University students, the ghosts of three Yankee soldiers stumble around in the small structure in an eternal search for whiskey. The noisy revenants have been heard by many students, it is reported, who press their ears against the door of the building and listen carefully.

The story really begins in 1860, the year that Dr. Landon C. Garland, president of the University, turned the institution into a military school. It was not the threat of war which prompted this move but rather an effort to improve the behavior of the students. Many of the students had become wild and unruly, giving the school a bad reputation, and members of the University's board of trustees hoped that the imposition of military discipline would curtail their boisterousness.

So in 1860, the University of Alabama took on all the trappings of a military academy with uniforms, titles, regulations, and such. There was a new building on the campus that year, an octagonal sentry box built of grey stone, for the use of students on guard duty.

Before the 1860-1861 school year ended, many of the University students had exchanged the uniform of college for the uniform of the Confederate States of America. In June 1861 the admission age for students was lowered to fourteen in an effort to keep the loss of the military-age students from drastically depleting the enrollment.

And so the young University cadets drilled and saluted and stood guard duty, and what had begun as a maneuver to curb youthful pranks changed, as the war progressed, into a serious exercise for survival.

It was early April 1865 when news reached the University that General John T. Croxton and his Federal troops were on their way to Tuscaloosa. There had been earlier reports of skirmishes between Croxton's forces and Confederate units, and there had been accompanying reports of the destruction left behind by the victorious Yankees.

Croxton's raiders had split from General J. H. Wilson's main forces, and while the troops under Wilson's command set out to destroy the Confederate arsenal and shipyards in Selma, Croxton was ordered to capture Tuscaloosa.

The alarm was sounded very early (only a little past midnight) on the morning of April 4 that advance units of the Yankee invaders were crossing the covered bridge over the Warrior River between Northport and Tuscaloosa.

Colonel J. T. Murphee, commander of the cadets, hastily

assembled his sleepy troops and addressed them briefly:

"Gentlemen," he said, "the Federal troops are on the outskirts of Tuscaloosa. We will do what we can to protect the city and our school."

Then off the cadets marched to pit their youthful dedication against the experience, the superior weapons, and the overwhelming numerical forces of the enemy. Even against such odds the University cadets did not do badly: they inflicted twenty-three casualties among Croxton's men before Colonel Murphee ordered them to retreat to the campus. Three University students were wounded during the engagement.

Waiting for the retreating cadets was Dr. L. C. Garland who joined them on a march to Marion. When they paused to rest along the banks of Hurricane Creek, Dr. Garland led the group in prayer for divine strength and guidance during the days ahead.

Not all the University cadets, the story goes, accompanied Dr. Garland to Marion: at least two young men stayed on the campus. Nobody recalls their names—if the names were ever known.

"We are not going to run away," they are reported to have said. "We're going to stay here and kill us some Yankees."

They had a plan. One of them hid in the sentry box, the Round House. The other young student strolled about the campus nearby.

It was hot inside the Round House with the long green shutters closed, but the youth hidden there needed the protection of the semi-darkness. By peeping through the slats in the blinds, he could watch some of the activity on the campus. He saw Professor Delorffe, the librarian, in earnest conversation with a Yankee officer. Later he learned that the librarian had been pleading to have the library and its treasury of books spared. General Croxton (he was only twenty-seven years old) replied that his orders were to burn the University, all of it, even the books. One volume was spared from the collection in the library, a copy of the Koran.

The hidden cadet heard the order, "Fire the building!" and he watched in helpless anger as soldiers tossed lighted torches through the doors and windows of the library.

The Round House,
now known as Jason Shrine,
looks much the same today as it did in 1865.

It was while the library was burning that he saw three Yankees approach his friend and heard them ask:

"Fellow, is there any whiskey on this campus? We are mighty thirsty!"

"Yes, sir," the Southern student answered with exaggerated politeness. "Yes, sir! The cadets always kept some whiskey hidden in the Round House, that little grey building over there. I think the door's unlocked."

The thirsty trio hurried to the Round House, snatched open the door and entered. Before their eyes could adjust to the subdued light inside the building, the waiting student stepped from his hiding place and shot all three of them.

Nobody heard those three shots, for at that very instant the powder magazine, ignited by the Yankee soldiers, exploded with a thunderous roar that shook the countryside.

The cadet slipped out of the Round House and joined his companion. The two of them made good their escape before the bodies of the invaders were discovered.

That's the story they tell on the University of Alabama campus.

Later, campus historians have recorded, ashes from each of the burned buildings were heaped near the Round House and buried beneath a mound of earth. A boulder nearby was dedicated to the memories of the University of Alabama cadets who resisted the advance of the Federal forces into Tuscaloosa. One of those cadets was seventeen-year-old Braxton Bragg Comer who in 1907 became governor of Alabama.

The names of the two students connected with the legend of the Round House are not recorded, of course, nor are the names of their victims.

The Round House looks much the same today as it did that April day in 1865. Nobody quite understands why it, the only real military building on the campus, was not burned; but it, together with the president's mansion, the observatory, and Steward's Hall (Gorgas House) escaped the rampage of the arsonists.

The former sentry box has a new name and a new purpose. It is known now as Jason Shrine, and it is used by members of the Jasons, senior men's honorary, for occasional meetings, for storing the organization's memorabilia, and for ceremonies connected with the tapping of new members.

Those ceremonies used to border on violence: a student chosen for membership was notified of his honor by being knocked down by a stalwart Jason, a painful ritual that began soon after the organization was formed in 1914. In later years, the rites were toned down so that, instead of being lambasted, the new member was doused with a bucket of soapy water as official notification of his selection.

Such boisterous activities might be expected to exorcise all restless spirits from the historic building, but, University students maintain, the ghosts of the three thirsty Yankee soldiers remain active there.

And through the years the tradition of "listening for the Yankees" has continued as students press their ears against the door of Jason Shrine, hoping to hear three Yankee ghosts rummaging about in their eternal search for whiskey.

Granny Dollar And Her Dog

Southern folklore is enlivened by many tales of animal ghosts, particularly ghosts of dogs, but perhaps none is more loyal than the ghost of Buster, the mongrel dog that belonged to Granny Dollar up in DeKalb County.

Some people who live around Mentone say that not only the ghost of Buster but also the ghost of Granny Dollar herself lingered many years around the ruins of her mountain cabin. They saw her ghost, neighbors said, sitting on the steps of the cabin, and they heard the old woman calling her dog long after they both were dead. Other folks told of hearing Granny talk in the high-pitched range she used when she conversed with her pet brown hen. It was an eerie sound, they said. Gave them the creeps.

Those tales may be true. For if, as serious students of folklore maintain, the spirit of the deceased sometimes returns to right a wrong, then Granny Dollar's spirit had cause for returning: callous thieves stole the pittance she had saved to buy a tombstone for her grave. Granny Dollar was tough and fearless and straightforward, and it is unlikely that she would rest quietly in her unmarked grave after such an act of thievery.

That theft occurred a day or so after Granny Dolllar's death in January 1931, and some people, former neighbors, said the old woman's ghost became active almost immediately.

Even without a ghost story about her, Granny Dollar is a legendary figure in DeKalb County.

Granny achieved notoriety by living to be at least one hundred eight years old—and probably older. But it is more than mere longevity that brought attention to Granny: those years were filled with memorable activity.

She was part Indian, daughter of a Cherokee Indian (a giant of a man who passed his physical characteristics along to his daughter) named William Callahan and a half-Cherokee, half-Irish mother named Mary Sexton Callahan. She gloried in her Indian heritage.

The site of her birth was on Sand Mountain at a place called Buck's Pocket, a spot destined to become famous more than a century later as a haven for defeated Alabama politicians. Her parents named her Nancy. The exact date of her birth is undocumented, but it seems to have been about 1826. She was old enough to recall details of the sad removal of the Indians to the West in 1835. Years later, Nancy used to tell how her family hid in caves to escape being sent away from their home. Nancy, being young and fleet-footed, slipped out of the hiding places during the night to scavenge food. It was she who spied on the dreaded military men and who brought word to her parents when it was safe for them to leave the cave and return home.

The family had moved to Georgia, and she was in her mid-thirties when the War Between the States began.

Granny walked for miles through the woods, stopping often to admire the beauty of De Soto Falls.

That war, they said, broke Nancy's heart.

She was not a pretty woman, not the kind a man would likely choose for a wife. Men respected her and maybe even envied her strength (she could run for miles without wearying, and, more practically, she could plow all day and half the night—straight furrows, too), but no man had asked her to marry him.

It was not merely her size (she was more than six feet tall) that discouraged suitors. Even as she was growing up, there was talk about Nancy (nobody called her Granny then, of course) that set her apart, marked her as different. There were reports that Nancy was a conjure woman and that she could foretell the future. In her old age, she did make a little money telling fortunes for strangers who came to see her, but this gift of prophecy served to set her apart in her youth.

And some people claimed Nancy could talk to the animals in their own languages, that she could walk into the woods and purely carry on conversations with foxes and squirrels and deer and such. Maybe that was true. Nancy, being raised Indian, was an expert woodsman who was familiar with animals and their habits, and she felt at home in the forests.

An Indian man might have understood Nancy's closeness to wild things, but the young Indian man had been banished to the far West. And the white men who knew Nancy were uncomfortable, uneasy, around her.

So Nancy watched her brothers and sisters (there were twenty-five of them) grow up and marry and have children to love and to brag about. Nancy helped with the births of some of those children (she was an experienced midwife), and she loved them all. If she was envious, she never mentioned it. Nancy was too busy to indulge in self-pity.

Soon after the family moved to Georgia, Nancy began operating a sort of pioneer delivery service. She set up her headquarters in the family home, near what is now Atlanta, and hauled merchandise to country stores within a radius of some thirty miles.

The wholesale dealer had barrels of molasses, kegs of whiskey, bags of salt, wagon wheels, gun powder, lead, boots, cured meat, and other goods loaded onto Nancy's wagon (actually Nancy did most of

Nancy did most of the loading herself, and tales of her "unnatural" strength were added to the other stories told about her.

the loading herself, and tales of her "unnatural" strength were added to the other stories told about her, further discouraging any courtships).

Those stories of her strength also discouraged thieves and bandits from bothering Nancy. Though she traveled alone, often at night, through isolated and rough country with valuable goods in her mule-drawn wagon, Nancy was never molested or robbed.

One of the stores on Nancy's route was owned by a prosperous merchant named Porter. She had been making deliveries there for several years when local loafers, men who spent a lot of time sitting around the store whittling and telling tales, began to tease Porter's son, Thomas, about being sweet on Nancy.

"Look a-yonder," they'd say. "Tom's a-helpin' that Indian woman tote the stuff offen her wagon and into the store. Looks like Tom's done fell in love with a BIG Indian!" And they'd laugh at their own crude humor.

Tom pretended he didn't hear. Nancy ignored the rough remarks, but she did wonder how Tom felt about her.

"You don't have to help me," she said to him one day when he came out of the store to heft a barrel off her wagon. "I can manage."

"I want to help," Tom replied. And he smiled at her in a way no man had ever smiled at her before. "And don't pay any mind to them," he added, staring hard at the teasing men on the store porch.

It must have been several months later that Tom finally asked Nancy to marry him. Some folks said he had to get his father's permission (it was reported that old man Porter threatened at first to disinherit Tom and even to throw him out of the house and store if he married "that Indian woman") before he could talk of marriage. But he did ask her, asked her properly, and Nancy accepted. She was happier than she had ever been.

The time wasn't right for happiness though, not for Nancy Callahan or for anyone else in the South. The War Between the States snatched away a thousand dreams of happiness.

Nancy's father, overage but patriotic, joined the Confederate forces and was killed in the Battle of Atlanta, and Thomas Porter also gave his life for the Confederacy. The two men whom Nancy loved, the only men who had ever loved her, were dead.

But there was not time to grieve. Sheman and his troops came riding through her cornfield, and Nancy watched in helpless anger as the soldiers stripped row after row of the young roasting ears from the tall stalks and then trampled the rest of the corn under the feet of their horses. In later years, when she was asked how she managed to survive those dreadful times, Nancy's only reply was, "I am an Indian." She did not like to talk about those years.

But she did survive, she and the young brothers and sisters—and their children—who were still in her care. Some time after the war ended, she moved back to northeast Alabama and turned again to farming.

Years passed. Nancy, an older Nancy, was a familiar figure on Lookout Mountain. Her neighbors watched her go into the woods and wander in Little River Canyon in search of roots, berries, leaves, and bark to use in concocting her Indian medicines. And when they were sick, those neighbors often sent for Nancy to doctor them with the native "cures" she had learned as a child.

Perhaps it was about that time that people began to refer to her as Granny. It was not merely her age that prompted the title; it was her practice of folk medicine, especially her practice of midwifery. Granny delivered many a baby on Lookout Mountain. But she never had one of her own.

Old age did not seem to lessen Granny's strength and vigor (she walked as tall and straight as she always had, and she continued to cultivate her land, to gather herbs, and to doctor the ailing), but she was lonely. With her parents dead and her brothers and sisters gone, Nancy—Granny—had time for loneliness, time to lament the loss of the happiness she might have had.

And then, wonder of wonders, love came again to Granny. She was in her late seventies ("Entirely too old for such foolishness," the neighbors whispered) when she married Nelson Dollar. He was a few, maybe half a dozen, years younger than Granny.

Though some folks laughed at the marriage of the old couple and reckoned they didn't have long to spend together, the marriage seems to have been a happy one for both of them. And it lasted for twenty years, until Nelson Dollar died in 1923 at the age of ninety-two.

During their married life, they never had any money, but they had a roof over their heads and they raised the food they needed. They got along.

Nelson was never able to buy nice things for Granny, though he used to entertain her by listing all the fine presents he would give her if he had the money to buy them.

Probably the only real present he ever gave her was a puppy, a little cur dog from a litter nobody wanted.

"I brought you a fine surprise," he told her as he held the scrawny puppy out to her.

Nancy took the squirming bundle of fur in her arms and stroked it with her rough hands. The puppy lifted his head and licked Granny on her chin.

"He must like you," Nelson laughed. "He kissed you."

"I like him," Granny replied. "He's a fine dog. I am going to name him Buster."

Buster became Granny's constant companion and guardian, seldom letting her out of his sight. Occasionally Nelson would tease Granny about Buster. "You love that dog better than you do me," he would say. "I never should have brought him to you!" And they would both laugh.

After Nelson died, laughter left Granny's cabin.

Granny grieved over the death of her husband. The cabin was quiet and lonely without him, and she turned more and more to Buster for the companionship and comfort she needed.

"Nelson gave me the only living thing that really loves me," Granny tried to explain to a neighbor, "and I never gave him a thing. It troubles me. I never gave him a present, and now it is too late."

But it wasn't too late. Granny did give Nelson a present. She sold the only cow she had to get money to pay for a tombstone for Nelson Dollar's grave. The simple granite marker, bearing his name and the dates of his birth and death, was placed at his grave in Little River Cemetery. After the marker was in place, Granny somehow felt better.

"I've given him a fitting present now, one that will last a long time. I think he'd like it," she said as she ran her hand over the lettering cut into the stone.

It may have been about that time that Granny began saving for her own tombstone. She had no family to care about marking her grave, and her neighbors, most of them, were as poor as she was.

So, whenever she had one to spare, Granny tucked a dollar bill (they were the old, big kind) away in a trunk in her cabin. Some of those dollars she earned by selling vegetables from her garden. Some of them were given to her by grateful ncighbors whose ailments she had cured or whose babies she delivered. And some of the dollars were gifts from visitors who came to see the "quaint old Indian woman" and to have their fortunes told.

Granny read palms, foretold the future by the lines in the hand. After she had welcomed her visitors and had made certain that Buster would bite no one, Granny would take a battered pocket knife out of her apron, open it, and trace the lines in the hand of her visitor with the tip of the blade while she disclosed events of the future.

Just how expert Granny was at this fortunetelling is uncertain, but her personality and her appearance combined to attract summer residents and tourists to her cabin. Some of their contributions went into her trunk to increase her tombstone fund.

She never worried about thieves stealing her money because she knew Buster would protect it. Buster had a widespread reputation as a vicious dog.

Once she had put a dollar bill into the trunk (she kept them wrapped in blue tissue paper), no emergency was great enough to induce her to take it out. She'd go hungry before she would spend her tombstone money.

If she got too hungry, Granny would make the rounds of her neighbors, offering them an opportunity to put some food in the sack she carried with her. They, poor though they were, shared whatever they had.

"If you don't help me, I'll have to go to the poorhouse," Granny would say. The fear of being a ward of the poorhouse haunted Granny. So her neighbors did what they could to help her hold on to her independence and remain in her own home.

Those same neighbors came to nurse her in her final illness when an accumulation of fluid in her body made it impossible for her to care for herself any longer.

Shortly before she died, Granny asked two of her friends to open her trunk and count her money for her. They found twenty-three dollar bills wrapped in the blue paper. Granny was satisfied. "That will do," she said. "That will buy me a tombstone." She watched as the bills were rewrapped and put back into the trunk.

A few days later, a cold January day in 1931, she died.

Friends remembered one of her last requests, and a strange request it was. Granny asked that a dance be held in her cabin before she was buried. So, though they considered it a peculiar, almost sacrilegious request, they recognized that the death dance was a part of Granny's Indian tradition, and they carried out her wishes.

Her cabin was small, so they had to move her bed to make room for the dancers around her corpse. Then they danced, danced for Granny.

Contributions from the community paid for the oak lumber used to build her coffin, and Colonel Milford Howard persuaded DeKalb

County oficials to pay five dollars for a hearse to transport the body to Little River Baptist Church. Colonel Howard also delivered the eulogy.

After the funeral services, after Granny Dollar had been buried beside her husband in the windswept country churchyard, the friends returned to her home to give it a final cleaning.

Buster was waiting for them. He was old and toothless and nearly blind, but he growled and snarled and charged at everyone who tried to approach him. The mountaineers held a conference and decided that Buster would die of grief and starvation if he were left at the cabin—and he seemed determined to stay there. Chloroforming the faithful old dog was the kindest thing they could do, it was agreed, and so Buster was mercifully killed.

There was a funeral for Buster, too, and once again Colonel Howard delivered a eulogy.

Perhaps it was while friends were attending Buster's burial that thieves entered Granny's cabin. With the faithful dog no longer there to thwart them, they boldly ransacked the place, emptying the trunk, tearing open the cornshuck mattresses, and scattering Granny's meager possessions across the floor.

They stole the twenty-three dollars Granny had saved to buy a tombstone for her grave.

Shortly after that theft, people passing the cabin at night began to tell of seeing the ghost of a woman, a large woman, prowling around the premises.

"It's Granny Dollar," they said. "She's looking for her tombstone money. She set a store on having her grave marked, and it looks like she can't rest until it's done. Her spirit just can't stay in an unmarked grave."

For years the sightings continued, and each time there was a new report of a restless spirit roaming around Granny Dollar's cabin, somebody would tell again of how determined Granny was to have a proper marker at her grave.

Finally, in 1973, Mrs. Annie Young of Fort Payne asked for contributions to buy a tombstone for Granny Dollar. People who knew her, or knew about her, gave money for the project (it cost considerably more than the twenty-three dollars Granny had saved), and on January 31, 1973, the marker was placed at her grave.

There have been no reports of anyone's seeing Granny Dollar's ghost since that day.

But Buster's ghost is still around. People passing the ruins of Granny's cabin late at night tell of hearing a low growl and warning barks, as though a faithful dog were guarding something—or someone—he loved.

Sudden Laughter

It is no wonder that Colonel Jerry Doherty fell in love with Lowndesboro: the gentle beauty of the antebellum village has captured many hearts.

Colonel Doherty came upon Lowndesboro rather unexpectedly one day in the spring of 1974. Stationed at Maxwell Air Force Base in Montgomery, he was approaching retirement and wanted to find an old house, a fine old house, to restore for use as a dwelling and as a location for catering private parties. He had found nine houses that appealed to him in and around Montgomery, but a variety of complications (potential demolition for interstate highway rights-of-way, inability to get clear title, disagreement among heirs, etc.) prevented his buying any of them.

He was becoming discouraged about finding the right house and was considering returning to California when, on a Sunday afternoon drive, he discovered Lowndesboro. He turned off Highway 80 between Montgomery and Selma, and drove down a winding road, a road linking proud old houses like gems on a twisting chain.

He drove slowly past the homes, the churches, the post office, the store, and he pulled into a driveway to turn around. At the end of that driveway, in a yard bright with jonquils, hyacinths, and flowering shrubs, stood a graceful house with slender Doric columns across the front and a wide front door that seemed to invite and welcome guests.

"That is my house," Colonel Doherty said aloud. "My house."

So he made inquiries and found that the house, known as Marengo, was managed by the Lowndesboro Landmarks Foundation and might possibly be available for leasing. It had been damaged by a recent tornado, he was told, and was badly in need of repair. His informant was about to tell him the history of the house, but Colonel Doherty was not interested in history—not then. All he wanted was to be able to move into Marengo, repair it, and open his business.

There were delays, as there often are in such transactions, but in the fall of 1974, Colonel Doherty and his wife, Allison, moved into Marengo.

"We were glad to be in the house," Colonel Doherty recalls, "but I felt uneasy there. I thought at first the feeling came because the house had been damaged and was not secure, that it was too easy for intruders to enter the place.

"But even after we had completed the major repairs and had made the house as burglarproof as such a house can be, the uneasiness continued. I slept with my pistol near me each night though deep down I sensed that whatever it was that gave me this uncomfortable sense of foreboding could not be shot—not with an ordinary pistol. But I still kept that weapon nearby."

While he was still trying to analyze his feeling of uneasiness, he was diverted by the recurring sound of laughter, sudden laughter, as

At the end of the driveway stood a graceful house with slender Doric columns across the front.

though a woman were laughing over a happy surprise.

Sometimes Colonel and Mrs. Doherty would be awakened by the sudden laughter of an unseen woman. At other times, busy with the continuing work of repairing Marengo, they would hear the laughter coming from another part of the house.

Though the laughter was quite distinct and though they hurried to the rooms where the sounds seemed to come from, they never found anyone—or anything—in the house.

"We tried to tell ourselves that it was the wind we heard whistling around this old house," Colonel Doherty recalls, "but winds moan; they don't produce the happy sound of laughter. And the sounds we heard were happy, very definitely the sounds of a woman laughing about something that pleased her very much."

But though the sounds were happy, they still disturbed the Dohertys, as the unknown always tends to disturb logical human beings.

There was a feeling, too, that someone, someone unseen, was in the house with them, the feeling that they were being watched by eyes they could not see.

Visitors to Marengo confessed to experiencing the same sensations, the awareness of an unseen presence and the feeling of being closely watched. Mrs. Doherty's mother, for example, came for a visit but was so upset by the "strange feeling" she had in Marengo that she refused to sleep there.

It was as this point that Jerry Doherty became extremely interested in learning more about the history of the house he and his wife occupied. He started by asking the postmaster, a longtime resident named Mrs. Dorothy Howard. He did not wish to appear foolish nor did he wish to start any rumors about ghosts, so one day when he stopped by the post office to mail a letter, he chatted for a few minutes and then asked casually,

"Is there anything unusual about Marengo? Anything I should know about?"

Mrs. Howard chuckled. "We've been wondering when you would ask about the ghost," she replied. "You've heard her, haven't you?"

Jerry Doherty was relieved, relieved to learn that there was a ghostly legend surrounding Marengo, that he and Allison had not conjured up the strange feelings of an unseen presence nor merely imagined that they had heard sudden laughter.

From conversations with natives of Lowndesboro, from scattered records, and from local histories, Jerry and Allison Doherty pieced together the story of Marengo and of the ghostly laughter there. This is what they learned from their research:

The house originally stood across the Alabama River, north of Lowndesboro, in Autauga County where it was built by Dr. John Howard in 1835. After his family had lived in the house for several years, Dr. Howard became dissatisfied with its location. The area had not prospered or grown as he had thought it would, and it did not offer the opportunities for professional and cultural advancements he had expected.

Lowndesboro, on the other hand, was a thriving community with good schools and strong churches, and it was a place where his medical skill would be in greater demand.

Dr. Howard would likely have moved immediately except for one thing: he liked the home he had built in Autauga County, and he did not want to leave it. So he decided to take it with him.

Board by board and brick by brick he had his servants dismantle the house. Each brick and each board was numbered so that the house could be reconstructed at its new site exactly the way it was originally built.

The materials were floated across the river on rafts to Newport Landing, then hauled by oxteams to its present site and rebuilt there. The date is placed at 1843 by some historians and 1847 by others.

Dr. Howard did change the house slightly, making an outside door from one of the windows that flanked the fireplace in a front room. The door, he explained, was placed there for the convenience of his patients, to give them easy access to his office.

This office, where first Dr. Howard and later Dr. Charles Edwin Reese treated their patients, played a role in saving Lowndesboro from destruction by Wilson's Raiders during the final days of the

War Between the States.

After the ravage of Selma in April 1865, General Wilson's troops marched toward Montgomery. Lowndesboro lay in their path, and citizens feared that their homes and churches would be vandalized and burned, just as homes and churches in Selma had been destroyed. As the Federal forces neared Lowndesboro, it chanced that Dr. Reese had a patient in his office, that office in his home, whose face was broken out with an angry rash.

Taking that patient with him, Dr. Reese rode out to meet the Yankees. He requested and was given an interview with General Wilson. After introducing himself, the doctor said:

"General, I feel I must warn you that there is smallpox in Lowndesboro. Your men will occupy that town at great personal risk to their health."

He motioned to the young man who had accompanied him. "This is one of my patients," he said.

General Wilson, from a safe distance, looked hard at the bumps and splotches on the man's face. Then to the doctor he said,

"Take that man away. And I thank you for your warning. I will not subject my men to the possibility of catching that disease. We will avoid your town."

So, though the Yankees did camp in a grove near the town and though there persist accounts of sporadic raiding by some troops, Lowndesboro was not destroyed.

Whether or not Dr. Reese's patient actually had smallpox has never been definitely determined.

These and other stories of Lowndesboro and of his home Colonel Doherty learned as he delved into the history of the place.

Dr. Reese's family, Colonel Doherty was told, lived in the home (they called it Jasmine because of the luxuriant Cape Jasmine bushes growing in the yard) until Mrs. Sarah Dudley Reese's death in 1924.

It was Mrs. Reese, according to local tradition, who had a massive brass lock, a lock still in place, installed on the front door. She was frightened at being left in the isolated house when Dr. Reese was called out to see his patients at night, and she continuously nagged and berated him for leaving her there unprotected.

"You are more concerned about your patients than about the safety of your own wife! You care more about them than you do about me!" she accused him.

So the big brass lock with its big brass key was put on the front door. Mrs. Reese, they said, kept that key with her at all times. And there were reports, never verified, that she, in fits of anger, sometimes used it to lock her husband out.

L. James Powell bought the property in 1925, and it was he who named the house Marengo, honoring the southwest Alabama county where his wife had grown up.

L. James Powell, Jr., inherited Marengo in 1959, becoming master of the house where he had grown to manhood, the house he loved.

Jimmy was a talented, charming man, friends told Colonel Doherty. He was an artist, musician, writer, lover of books, and delightful conversationalist. Yet he drifted from one occupation to another, always seeking, never satisfied. His one obsession was to restore Marengo.

His wife, Kathleen, shared his devotion to Marengo.

Kathleen Powell, Colonel Doherty was told, was an unusual woman. She was an invalid when Jimmy met and married her, unable to walk because of injuries suffered in an accident. She could get about a bit on crutches, but she spent most of the time in a wheel chair.

As had other women before her, Kathleen disliked being left alone at Marengo. So Jimmy bought her a pistol and taught her how to use it. He pushed her chair out onto the back porch at Marengo and showed her how to aim and fire at targets in the yard. Kathleen was an apt pupil.

One night in 1961, after Kathleen's maid had put her to bed, Jimmy drove the woman home in his pickup truck. He returned to Marengo and found Kathleen lying on a blood-drenched pillow.

"Come quickly," he telephoned friends. "Kathleen has shot herself." She died a few hours later.

113

The death was ruled suicide, but there were questions, ugly questions, as there often are when prominent people are involved in tragedy.

Kathleen left her husband a "substantial sum" of money, some reports say as much as half a million dollars. It was enough money to restore Marengo, but though extensive work was done on the house, Jimmy Powell's interest in the project was diverted. Before long, the money was gone.

In 1971 Marengo was sold to Colonel (retired) amd Mrs. Robert Simpson. It was later sold to Mr. and Mrs. William Cabiness of Birmingham who turned it over to the town of Lowndesboro.

Jerry Doherty studied the history of the house, thought of the people who had lived there, and wondered. That sudden laughter—whose was it?

He and Allison established The Marengo Tea House in their home, and Jerry, when asked to do so, often entertained their guests by telling them of the history of Marengo and of the strange happenings, the sudden laughter, there. Some guests even claimed they heard the laughter, but Jerry was never sure they did.

One night in the fall of 1975, a group from Maxwell came out to have dinner at Marengo. Among the guests was Sylvia C., a psychic from New York, who was visiting friends at the air force base. There was no talk of ghosts or of haunting that night, only a brief, almost stylized, account of the early years of the house.

After dinner, the guests were assembled in the downstairs bar, and Jerry was standing behind the cash register there. Sylvia, who had been quiet almost to the point of being withdrawn all evening, walked around to him and said softly:

"Jerry, you know you and Allison are not alone in this house."

He was surprised, but he curbed his desire to question her, thinking he might give her information she could use in what could be mere speculation. He knew she had never been in the house before and that she had no knowledge of the people who had lived in it through the years.

"There is a presence here, a woman named Kathleen," the

114

Mrs. Reese, they say, kept this big brass key to the front door of her home (now Marengo) with her at all times.

psychic continued. "She was born in February, she died in February, and her spirit will leave this house in February."

The psychic added that Jerry and Allison had made Kathleen happy, thus freeing her spirit. "The beauty and the love and the happiness you have brought to Marengo have given her peace and joy. You two are living here the kind of life she dreamed of living. Because of you, her spirit is free to leave."

Jerry pondered the words he had heard. He put his hand in his jacket pocket and felt the big front door key. On impulse, he laid it on the bar.

Sylvia recoiled and threw up her hands. "Don't put that key near me," she said loudly. "It has an evil charge."

The other guests, attracted by the commotion, congregated around Sylvia and Jerry. They saw Sylvia point to the key and say, "It belonged to a woman who was very unhappy here, a woman whose name was --" She hesitated a moment. "Whose name was Sarah. Sarah Dudley?"

The rest of the evening was spent discussing Sarah Dudley Reese and Kathleen Powell and Marengo and ghosts and sudden laughter.

As the guests were leaving, Sylvia said again, "Kathleen will leave Marengo in February."

The latter part of January 1976 Jerry and Allison Doherty left Lowndesboro on an extended vacation to California and Hawaii. It was the last day of February when they returned to Marengo.

As they entered the house, they were immediately aware of a feeling of peace and tranquillity such as they had never experienced before.

And never again have they heard that strange, sudden laughter.

The Ghosts At Montevallo's Mansion House

Nobody at Kingswood took her seriously when Julia first reported seeing ghostly lights bobbing around in the family burying ground near the King house. She claimed it was Marse Edmund's ghost.

"Now, Aunt Julia, you know you didn't see ghost lights near the graveyard. Maybe you saw a lot of lightning bugs out there," Elizabeth King Shortridge said, trying to reason with the old woman, when Julia brought the story to her. "And surely you know that Papa—Marse Edmund—wouldn't be out there roaming around his grave!" she added sharply. Then, to ease the sting of her tone, she said gently, "You miss him, too, don't you?"

"Yessum," Julia replied. "I misses him. He was a good man. Stayed here a long time; a long time the Lord spared him. But his spirit has done come back. I seed him. Wasn't no lightning bugs!" she snorted. "Marse Edmund's ghost is out there taking care of the money he hid."

"Now, Aunt Julia—," Elizabeth Shortridge began. Then she stopped. Why try to reason with the superstitious woman? So, instead of continuing the conversation, she dismissed Julia by saying, "Please go out to the kitchen and see if there's any clabber. I think I'd like some for supper."

As she watched Julia cross the outside passageway to the kitchen, Elizabeth sighed and ran her hand across her forehead. "Ghosts! We have enough sorrow and disruption here already. I don't believe I can cope with stories of ghosts!" It was 1863. Wartime.

But the stories continued, similar stories of sightings of moving lights, like a man carrying a lantern, out in the orchard back of the house and along the walk that led to the family cemetery. And the tellers, almost without exception, ended their accounts with, "It's old Marse Edmund out there guarding his buried treasure."

The Marse Edmund they referred to was Edmund King, the builder of Kingswood and its master for forty years.

Born in Virginia in 1782, Edmund King was thirty years old when he married Nancy Ragan in Griffin, Georgia. Their son, William Woodson, and the new year of 1813 arrived simultaneously, and two years later a daughter, Louisa, was born.

Edmund King possessed an adventuresome and ambitious spirit (his friends all predicted that he would become a very rich man), and life in the small Georgia town was too confining for him. He had heard accounts of rich lands available to settlers in the Alabama Territory, and he determined to explore the frontier.

Taking two of his servants with him, he went to the seaport city of Mobile. There he made arrangements to go up the Alabama River near the site of Cahawba where his cousin, William Rufus King, later organized a land company. This may have been where Edmund had originally intended to settle (his cousin believed strongly in the future prosperity of the area), but for some reason he decided to look further for a home site.

He and his two companions (family tradition says they were field hands, strong and healthy) rode on horseback from the present Dallas County northward through hilly, thickly wooded country to a community known as Wilson's Hill, some fifty miles away.

King liked the place, liked the streams, the hills, the trees. So he purchased huge tracts of land, and he and his servants built a hand-hewn log cabin on a gentle rise. When the cabin was finished, its roof on, and its chimney smoking, King looked at it and mused:

"It's not nearly as fine as our house in Georgia, but the walls are strong and the roof is tight, and it will do for a home for my family until I can build something better."

He set off for Georgia to bring his wife and little children to Wilson's Hill.

King had for his companion on this journey William Weatherford, the famous Indian warrior known as Red Eagle. The two men had met on the frontier and had become friends. Though their backgrounds and their experiences differed, they respected each other, and when Weatherford offered to help King move his family to its new home, King accepted gratefully. He felt safe in the company of Red Eagle.

When they arrived at Griffin, they packed the family's possessions into two covered wagons. Mrs. King, the two children, and a nurse rode in the family carriage while King and Weatherford scouted the route on horseback. Records show that fifteen slaves made the trip with the family.

If Nancy King was disappointed when she saw her frontier home, she hid her dismay and set about making it comfortable for her husband and children.

Before the year 1817 ended, there was another baby in the family, a girl named Elizabeth. Tradition says Elizabeth was the first white child born in the community that was later to become Montevallo.

Education was important to both Edmund and Nancy, and they were determined that their children, living in a wilderness though they were, should not grow up in ignorance or without culture. In addition to the family Bible, Nancy had brought from Georgia a blueback speller, a slender book familiar to students of that period, and when William was four years old, she taught him to read from the Scriptures and to spell common words from the speller. She taught him basic arithmetic by having him count the squares in her handmade quilts (they had been in her hope chest) and the patchwork on her aprons.

Then when he was only fourteen, William rode alone from Montevallo to Lexington, Kentucky, to enter Transylvania College, a journey that took him nearly a week. His clothes were packed in his saddlebags, and his money was tucked into a wide belt around his waist. His mother's early instruction had been sound: William graduated from college with first honors.

The other children (there were ten) were also well educated, though their mother played a smaller role in their instruction. As he grew more prosperous, Edmund King employed tutors for his children.

His prosperity manifested itself in another way. In 1823, six years after the family had settled in Alabama, Edmund King began building a permanent home, a dwelling suitable for a man of his position in the community.

The hewn-log structure, which had been improved and added to as the family grew, was replaced with a handsome brick building, two stories tall. The design was of the Federal style, rather austere, with an outside chimney at each end of the house. The inside walls were plastered and unadorned, the woodwork was plain.

Bricks for the house were made of clay from nearby Shoals Creek, shaped and baked in a kiln on the premises by artisans selected by the builder.

The windows, each flanked by wooden shutters, offered views of groves of cedars, oaks, and hickory trees and of the nearby orchard. It was, perhaps, the windows which attracted the greatest attention from King's neighbors: each window had real glass panes. Visitors came

Because of its imposing appearance, the King home was referred to as "the mansion house," but Edmund King called it Kingswood.

from miles around to see those clear glass windows, the first of their kind in that part of Alabama.

Because of its imposing appearance, the King home was referred to as "the mansion house," but Edmund King and his family preferred to call it Kingswood.

Edmund King was a leader in the religious, business, and social life of the new town. He was a devout Baptist and had helped in the organization of the oldest Baptist association in the state. In addition to his agricultural interests, he opened a mercantile store in Montevallo where he continued to make money. His home was known throughout the area as a place of gracious hospitality, and especially as a place where young people had a good time.

He hardly seemed the kind of man who, after his death, would be connected with tales of ghosts. And yet—

Even reports of his death are conflicting. Family accounts tell of failing health, increasing infirmities (he was eighty-two years old when he died on June 28, 1863), and a lingering illness.

Other accounts say that Edmund King was killed when he was struck on the head by a falling limb as he walked in his orchard at Kingswood. Yet another version, told by an elderly black man who grew up on the place, states that he died as a result of injuries suffered when he fell from a peach tree and landed on his head. Why (or how) he was climbing a peach tree was not explained.

It is known that Edmund King took pride in his fruit orchard and that, as he grew older, he walked among the trees there almost daily. Those walks took him also to the burying ground beyond the orchard where his beloved wife, Nancy, was buried (she died in 1842 at the age of forty-nine), and where the body of his young second wife, Susan Ward King (she died in 1850 after the couple had been married only two years) lay.

In that graveyard was also the body of his son, twenty-one-year-old Lyttleton, who was accidentally shot by one of his brothers while the two were hunting deer.

Edmund King walked often to that cluster of graves, and sometimes he lingered there so long, lost in a tangle of memories of times past, that his daughter, Elizabeth King Shortridge, had to send a servant to fetch him to meals. Elizabeth and her family had moved into Kingswood to care for her father when his health began to fail. They lived there during the War Between the States when Elizabeth's husband, Judge George Shortridge, and three of their sons (George Shortridge, Jr., Eli, and Frank) were serving in the Confederate Army. That conflict claimed the lives of those three sons.

Sometimes Edmund King wandered about the premises at night. Servants told of seeing him with a lantern and a shovel walking among the fruit trees after midnight. Some of them said he was cultivating those trees, a rather unusual occupation for that time of night. Others said he was burying his money so the Yankees couldn't find it.

Perhaps that report of buried money was responsible for accounts of sightings of ghostly lights ("I sho' seen Marse Edmund with his lantern, and he was walking like a natural man") that continued to be told after his death.

While the stories of the phantom lights continued, other stranger tales of the supernatural were told about Kingswood.

For many years, the children and grandchildren of the original occupants of Kingswood told of a ghost who haunted one of the upstairs bedrooms. The family members would be downstairs, sometimes gathered around the fireplace in the parlor, when they would hear in the room overhead the sound of someone getting out of a creaking bed and walking slowly across the floor.

The sounds were quite clear, they said, and their pattern never varied: always there was the distinctive noise of someone rising from bed and crossing the room with deliberate steps. People who heard it said the sounds were exactly like those made by Edmund King when he was old and spent much time resting in bed and walking slowly about in his bedroom.

Several family members tried to slip up on the ghost, but though the noises continued as they crept up the stairs, there was sudden silence as soon as they touched the door of the bedroom.

The ghostly sounds were not confined to nighttime hours but were frequently heard on quiet afternoons, as though the occupant of the empty room were waking up from a long nap.

And on stormy nights, they said, eerie lights would appear in the dark corners of that upstairs room, lights that would dart and dodge about as though defying anyone to approach them.

Uncle Frank, who had once been the personal servant of Frank King (youngest son of Edmund King), told an interviewer in Montevallo in 1913 of being sent upstairs on one occasion to investigate the noises. As he approached the dark bedroom, Uncle Frank said, he heard, "Clink-clink-clinkety-clink," not the sound of ghostly chains clinking but the sound of someone counting stacks of silver money.

When Uncle Frank struck a light to see who was counting the coins, the room was empty. No one was there. Nothing. But the sound of, "Clink-clink-clinkety-clink," continued.

Uncle Frank fled.

"I know it was Marse Edmund," he said. "I've seed him lots of times. He been hangin' around ever since he fell out of that peach tree and ceased to live. He protecting that money he hid around the place."

Aunt Julia and others agreed with Uncle Frank that the spectral lights seen so often between Kingswood and "that little lean, slim place of a graveyard" were guiding the ghost of old Marse Edmund to the money he had hidden.

But perhaps the strangest tale associated with Kingswood is the story of the wedding feast. Just whose wedding was being celebrated no one now recalls, but Kingswood was beautifully adorned for the event with greenery and candles and bells fashioned of white silk hanging from wide pleated streamers.

When the honorees and guests had assembled in the dining room for the meal, a servant brought in a large silver platter on which lay a whole roast pig with an apple in his mouth. A young girl, likely one of the wedding attendants, was selected to do the carving. As she drew the sharp knife across the roast pig, the pig squealed.

The guests departed from the room in terror, overturning chairs and goblets as they ran.

Once they were outside and had regained their composure, they were ashamed of their display of fear (they kept trying to reassure each other that they really had not heard the pig squeal, but secretly everyone was certain that a pig's squeal was exactly what they had heard), and they returned, somewhat hesitantly, to the table.

This time one of the groomsmen, a young man noted for his courage, volunteered to do the carving. He sharpened the knife blade and picked up the carving fork to hold the pig firmly on the platter while he sliced the meat. Everyone at the table stared straight at him. He was uncomfortable, apprehensive perhaps, but he was determined to show the assemblage that an ordinary roast pig could be carved in the ordinary way.

As he thrust the fork into the pig, a "huge white thing" crept from beneath the table, hovered between the bride and groom for an instant, and then vanished.

The supper went uneaten.

Later in the evening, when other guests joined the bridal party for dancing, the "huge white thing" reappeared. The guests saw what they described as a great white-robed figure outside the parlor door. The figure bounded lightly into the room, floated over the heads of the guests, whirled through an open window, and disappeared into the darkness.

The restless spirit of Edmund King was never in any way associated with this frightening visitation, but the event, they say, did occur in his fine house.

There was another story associated with Kingswood, one that might have happened somewhere else but supposedly happened right there.

One of the house servants, trusted and beloved by the family, had an unruly son. Though she scolded and punished and prayed, he continued his wild ways.

The boy delighted in tormenting his mother, and when he got provoked with her, he would call her bad names. He often shouted at her, "You're black as an old turkey buzzard—and just as ugly!" He was mighty unruly, had no respect for his elders.

The mother became very ill, and her friends hoped the boy would repent and change his ways and be good to his poor sick mama. But he didn't. In fact, he became more obstreperous than ever. One day, after he had been unusually bad, his mother pulled herself up in bed, looked straight at him, and declared, "Soon as I get able to get out of this bed,

I'm goin' to give you one mo' good whuppin'!''

Her unruly son just laughed and walked out of the room saying something about ''old black buzzard.''

The next day the mother died. They say her son never even shed a tear.

A few days later, the unruly son was walking along the edge of the woods behind Kingswood. Suddenly a big black buzzard swooped out of the sky and landed right on him. The buzzard beat him with her wings and clawed him with her feet until he was bloody all over.

Some folks say the buzzard gave the unruly son the ''good whuppin''' his mama had promised him.

Servants told of seeing Edmund King with a lantern and a shovel walking among the fruit trees after midnight.

The Locket

None of his descendants now knows why Jacob Hammer left his native Indiana and moved to Alabama. They do know from records in family Bibles that Jacob Hammer was living in Talladega County when he married Martha Louisa Hicks of Renfroe on December 1, 1887. He was thirty-four at the time of their marriage, and his bride was twenty-one.

Mr. Hammer had taught school and had been engaged in merchandising in Indiana, and family tradition says he taught school, ran a store, and farmed after he came to Alabama.

In the first six years of their marriage, five children were born to the couple: Cassandra, William Benjamin, Emma Everett, Diana, and Dixie Homer. Some of the children's names, family members point out, reflect Mr. Hammer's interest in Greek and Roman mythology. He was interested in many things. He wanted to call his first child by her full name, Cassandra, but his wife, who cared little for the classics, insisted on calling her Cassie, and Cassie she became.

Cassie was nine years old when her baby brother, Harvey, was born. She was a "big girl" then, old enough and responsible enough to take over much of the care of the new baby. Being the oldest in the family—and being a girl—Cassie at nine knew how to cook, clean house, wash clothes, iron, milk the cow, kill and dress a chicken, sew, mend and darn, and take care of the younger children.

They were living in the community of Stemley, near the Coosa River, in Talladega County then. All the children from Cassie to Harvey were born there, but the town has now dwindled into nothingness, and only a few older people remember where it was.

Cassie Hammer was likely too busy helping her mother care for the younger children, especially the baby, to have much time to play, but she really didn't mind. There was something different about taking care of Harvey, something that soothed her resentment over having the responsibilities of a grown-up forced so early upon her.

Harvey was a good baby. And he was beautiful.

"Look, Mama," Cassie would say after she had bathed and dressed him. "Look how beautiful Harvey is! I wish I had curly hair like he has. Look how it shines in the sunlight. And look how big his eyes are. Sometimes I think he sees things we can't see. What do you suppose he sees, Mama?"

Mrs. Hammer, being a sensible woman, replied, "Don't be silly, Cassie. He sees just what we see. Nothing else." She paused. "But he is a beautiful baby. I wish I could have his picture made looking just the way he looks now: all clean and shining and happy."

She took the baby in her arms and kissed him. It was not easy for Mrs. Hammer to show affection, wasn't her nature, but Harvey had a quality, an elusive quality that even his mother couldn't define, that called her to hug him and cuddle him and call him "my precious baby."

She took the baby in her arms and kissed him. It was not easy for Mrs. Hammer to show affection, wasn't her nature, but Harvey had a quality, an elusive quality that even his mother couldn't define, that called her to hug him and cuddle him and call him "my precious baby."

Everybody loved Harvey. They loved him not merely because he was the youngest in the family, but because Harvey himself was so loving. His arms went out to everyone who came near, his smile had a radiance of pure joy, and his laughter was as musical and refreshing as snatches of dancing tunes.

Even Jacob Hammer, usually too busy earning a living for his growing family to squander time in play, would bounce his baby on his knee and sing to him some half-forgotten songs from his Indiana boyhood, and talk to him about matters only the two of them understood.

"You know what?" Jacob asked his wife. "This son of ours will grow up to see flying machines carrying passengers and mail from city to city. And he'll ride on wide thoroughfares connecting the cities. Big changes are coming in this world—and Harvey will be part of them."

"O, Jacob!" Mrs. Hammer replied. "What a wild imagination you have! How do you ever think of such foolish things?"

"They're not foolish," Jacob stated firmly. "They'll come true. You'll see—if you live long enough. Harvey believes what I'm telling you. Don't you, Harvey?"

The baby smiled, and his eyes shone as though he did indeed understand, as though he shared with his father an exciting look into the future.

Harvey was walking and begining to talk a little when the family moved to Renfroe, a community some six miles west of Talladega. At that time, Mr. Hammer was devoting most of his energies to farming.

Cassie continued to be Harvey's loving protector, and the toddler adored her. Mrs. Hammer may have been a little jealous, but she tried not to show it.

"I hope your own babies will love you as much as Harvey does," she said to Cassie one day.

"He loves you, too, Mama," Cassie replied. "He loves everybody—but you most of all. Sometimes," she added, "I think it's not me but my gold locket that Harvey loves. He plays with it every time I wear it, and I believe he wants to wear it himself!"

Cassie's locket, her only piece of jewelry, had been a gift from her father. It was heart shaped and hung on a slender gold chain.

"It looks like you," Jacob Hammer had said as he fastened it around her neck. "It looks like my Cassandra."

Even then Harvey reached out to get the shining locket.

"No, Harvey," Cassie said gently. "Boys don't wear lockets. This is mine. Maybe some time I'll let you try it on. But not now!"

One stormy night in late September 1898 Cassie woke up and heard Harvey crying in her parents' bedroom. She ran across the hall and found her mother holding Harvey in her lap while Mr. Hammer rubbed the little boy's chest with melted tallow and wrapped a flannel cloth around him.

"It's the croup," Mrs. Hammer told Cassie. "He's real sick." She held the baby close and rocked him.

Harvey was limp and listless, and his breathing was raspy.

"What can I do?" Cassie asked.

"Nothing," Mrs. Hammer replied. "We've done all we can. Now we will just have to wait."

Just as daylight marked the end of that long night, Harvey Hammer died. He was twenty months old.

When word of the child's death spread through the community, the neighbors came, as they always came in the rural South. They were silent with grief, some of them, while others tried to speak comfortingly about "understanding some day" and "God's will." Jacob Hammer did not believe it was God's will for Harvey to die. Neither did Cassie.

The younger children walked around the house big-eyed and frightened until an aunt came to take them home with her.

Mrs. Hammer's grief was too deep for tears. "My baby. My precious baby," she kept repeating. "He's dead. And we don't even have a picture of him. We never had a picture made of our precious Harvey."

Mr. Hammer, hoping to ease his wife's sorrow, promised, "We'll send in to Talladega and get the photographer to come out and take Harvey's picture in his coffin. Then you—all of us—will have his picture to remember him by."

Outside, a cold, slashing rain seemed almost an extension of the gloominess of the household.

Men who lived nearby fashioned a small coffin from pine boards, and the women padded it with cotton and lined it with soft white cloth.

Those same neighbor women made a little dress for Harvey to be buried in. It was white, as befitted a burial garment for a pure child, and it had a wide, ruffled, lace-trimmed collar. When they put the garment on him, the neck was too big, making the collar hang low on his pale shoulders.

"That will be all right," one of the women said. "When we put him in the coffin, we'll just pull the collar in place and tuck the extra fullness under him."

And they did. After Harvey's body was placed in the coffin, and after the seamstresses had pulled up the collar and tucked it beneath him, nobody could tell the neck was too large.

"He looks so peaceful," the people said. "Just like he was asleep. Come look at your little brother, Cassie," they said.

Cassie looked. She knew the women were expecting her to say something, but she couldn't make any words come. She stood there silent for a long time, just looking at Harvey and wondering what it was like to be dead. Then, very slowly, she took off her heart-shaped locket and fastened it around Harvey's neck.

The rain never slacked.

Finally word came that the roads between Talladega and Renfroe were impassable, so the photographer couldn't come.

Harvey Hammer was buried without ever having had his picture made.

His mother continued to grieve, as did other members of the family, and she continued to weep over having no picture of her little boy.

"If only I had his picture to look at, to remember him by," she moaned.

A few weeks after Harvey's death, Mr. Hammer set out to clear a parcel of land some distance from his house. The land was too far away for him to go and come from home each day, so he made arrangements to camp in an abandoned one-room schoolhouse near the property. The building had a pot-bellied stove in it that he could use for heat and for cooking, so Mr. Hammer took a cot to sleep on, blankets, some food, and moved into the school.

The first night there, he was tired from the move and from the strenuous labor of clearing the land, and he fell asleep soon after he had eaten supper. He had been asleep for some time when he was awakened by a brilliant light.

His first thought was that the building was on fire, and he jumped up to run outside.

But as soon as he was fully awake, he realized that the building was not on fire. The light came from a corner of the room. In the corner was his little boy, Harvey, holding a burning candle.

Jacob Hammer walked toward the figure and reached out toward him. As he did, the child blew out the candle and vanished.

There was no more sleep for Jacob Hammer that night. Questions crowded in upon him: had he really seen his son or was his grief conjuring up cruel visions? Could Harvey have returned from the dead? And if so, why?

The daylight brought no answers, and the questions haunted him all the next day as he worked in his field.

That second night, the same thing happened: he was awakened by a flash of light and saw Harvey, holding a flickering candle, in the corner of the room. Once again Jacob Hammer approached the child, and once again the child blew out the candle and vanished.

As Jacob Hammer lay awake and tried to answer the questions that trampled through his mind, a new thought came to him. Was it possible, he wondered, that Harvey's spirit was so disturbed by his mother's yearning for a picture of him that he had come back so that such a picture could be made? The more he thought about it, the more he became convinced of the logic of his theory.

So when daylight came, instead of going to his field, Jacob Hammer went into Talladega to borrow a camera from W. H. McMillan, a photographer there.

He did not tell Mr. McMillan why he wanted to use the camera. He would have felt foolish saying that he intended to try to photograph a ghost, so he implied that he needed a picture of a landmark on his property, and he promised to return the camera early the next morning.

Mr. McMillan let him borrow one of the cumbersome old cameras with a tripod, and he showed him how to use it.

"Be careful with the glass negative," he warned. "They break right easy."

Jacob Hammer took the equipment back to the school building and set it up beside his cot, focusing it on the corner where he had seen the apparition on the two previous nights. He did not go to sleep that night: he sat on the side of the cot and waited.

Hours passed. Nothing happened. Mr. Hammer was beginning to wonder if he had imagined the whole thing when suddenly a bright light filled the room, and he saw Harvey in the far corner. He snapped the shutter of the camera, and the figure disappeared.

Mr. Hammer dozed fitfully (he was very tired) until daylight came. Then he went to Talladega to return the camera and to have the glass plate developed. Once again he wondered what he should tell the photographer, and once again he decided to tell him nothing.

After he had thanked the man for the use of the camera, he asked, "Will you please develop the plate? I took only one picture, but I would very much like to see it."

Jacob Hammer waited, a restless wait, until Mr. McMillan came out of the darkroom. He was holding the glass negative, still wet, up to the light.

"Jacob," he said, "I thought you did not have a picture of your little boy, the one who died."

"We don't have," Jacob Hammer replied.

"Yes, you do. This is him—Harvey—right here. Look."

Jacob Hammer looked. On the negative was the exact likeness of Harvey Hammer: blond curls, big eyes, wistful smile framed in a strange aura of light.

Jacob Hammer was unable to speak. He took the negative from the hands of the puzzled photographer and hastened home.

"Martha,! Martha!" he shouted as he ran into the house. "Look!" He held the glass negative up to the light.

On the negative was the exact likeness of Harvey Hammer: blond curls, big eyes, wistful smile, framed in a strange aura of light.

Martha Hammer looked and burst into sobs. "It's Harvey! It's my baby's picture!"

Cassie and the other children came running to see what was happening.

"It's Harvey!" they said. "Harvey. Just like he looked."

"And look," Cassie said, "look how his dress has fallen around his shoulders. And look around his neck—that's my heart-shaped locket, the one I put on him!"

After the family had seen the negative with the likeness of Harvey on it and after he had told the story of how he had made the picture, Jacob Hammer took the glass plate back to the photographer in Talledega to have prints made from it.

Three of those prints made in the fall of 1898 still exist. Each one, though faded by time, shows quite distinctly the head and shoulders of a beautiful blond child with wondering eyes that seem to peer into another world. The lace-trimmed collar of his white garment has slipped down around his shoulders. And round his neck hangs a gold, heart-shaped locket.

"Paint The Gallows Red"

"Tonight," Era Mae Barfoot promised herself, "I am going to sleep in Grandma's big bed."

The young girl shared a bedroom with her grandmother in the Barfoots' home in Troy, and though she did not mind sleeping on the day bed by the window, Era Mae welcomed the prospect of having the double bed all to herself while her grandmother was away on a visit.

And, perhaps, Era Mae thought, by sleeping in that bed she could find out why her grandmother so often rose at night, turned the drop light (it hung on a brown cord from the ceiling in the middle of the bedroom) on and off quickly, and then got back into bed.

The few times Era Mae had asked her Irish grandmother about the light, she never gave a direct answer, just talked vaguely about bad dreams and "seeing things" and such. To give an evasive answer was not like her grandmother, Elizabeth Jane Smith Cone, and the evasiveness bothered Era Mae. It bothered her, too, that her grandmother became so solemn, almost hostile, when Era Mae tried to question her about her unusual behavior. Grandmother Cone, a stout woman, normally had a resounding, carefree chuckle that punctuated her conversations, but she did not chuckle when Era Mae asked about the light. Something in her grandmother's manner made Era Mae quit asking. But she still wondered.

At bedtime that summer night in the early 1930s, Eva Mae decided to sleep with her head at the foot of the bed so that she would be cooled by any breeze that might blow through the open window. At first she tossed and tumbled from one side of the bed to the other, not from restlessness but from the delightful luxury of having room to move about freely. Soon, however, she fell into a sound sleep.

Later, Era Mae was never able to tell how long she had been asleep when she was awakened by the feeling that someone—or something— was in the room with her.

She opened her eyes and stared straight into the face of a man whose blazing dark eyes "burned a hole right in me."

Era Mae fainted.

When she aroused, the phantom visitor had disappeared.

Era Mae moved back into her own bed by the window, lay awake and wondered until daylight came. The girl did not tell her parents, Mr. and Mrs. Eugene Monroe Barfoot, about the intruder: they, she felt, would not believe her and would likely punish her for telling a falsehood. It was her grandmother she wanted to talk to.

So as soon as her grandmother returned from her overnight visit and the two of them were alone, Era Mae blurted out the account of her frightening experience. Her grandmother looked hard at Era Mae as she responded:

"Yes, I have seen him, too. Many times." Then came the explanation of why the old woman often rose to turn on the light at night.

"When I turn on the light, he goes away," she said. "I never wanted to talk about it, afraid your mama would think I'm crazy and old and might send me away."

For five years, from about 1932 to 1937, those strange visitations continued, and for five years grandmother and granddaughter kept their secret. Their sightings of the ghostly figure matched in every detail: he wore black pants and a white shirt, was well built, muscular as though he were accustomed to outdoor work, and had a high forehead and dark hair. But it was his eyes, those penetrating eyes that seared into the very soul, that were so fearsome.

His route never varied in all those years. Era Mae and her grandmother would hear him come from the living room, apparently from behind the piano, and fling open the French doors to the dining room. The gentle tinkling of the glasses on the buffet announced his passage, a board creaked, and a change in the steady hum of the electric refrigerator marked his progress. Then the door of their bedroom (the door was securely locked from the inside with a sliding bolt) would open, and he would stand at the foot of the big bed, not making a sound, just staring with those burning eyes.

After a moment or two (how can such fearful time be measured?), he would turn and retrace his steps. Era Mae and her grandmother would lie still and listen to the now-familiar pattern of sounds—the refrigerator's altered hum, the tinkling glasses, a squeaking board, the swinging French doors, and the footsteps in the living room. Then silence.

As the years passed, the initial fear that Era Mae and her grandmother had experienced was gone, replaced by a fleeting sadness, a vague awareness of some deep disturbance that enveloped the restless spirit that stalked their home. They wondered, though they never found the proper words to phrase their thoughts, what torturous memories, what unrelenting shackles to the past doomed the figure to an endless enactment of his ritualistic behavior.

Then one night the ghost changed his routine.

Era Mae was about sixteen years old. Her mother, after years of childlessness, had a baby. Mrs. Barfoot and the tiny baby were occupying the back bedroom, and Mr. Barfoot was sleeping in the guest room at the front of the house. He distributed cakes and cookies for the National Biscuit Company to stores throughout southeast Alabama, and he needed his sleep.

On this particular night, the spectre walked down the hall and entered Mrs. Barfoot's bedroom. When she saw the figure, Mrs. Barfoot shrieked with a piercing scream that aroused the household.

The figure vanished—instantly. By the time Mr. Barfoot, Mrs. Cone, and Era Mae reached the room, the phantom had disappeared, and Mrs. Barfoot was in hysterics.

Mr. Barfoot, thinking his wife was nervous from the strain of caring for the baby, tried to discount her story of the ghostly man who had stood at the foot of her bed and had stared at her with burning eyes.

"Now, now," he said soothingly. "It was nothing. Just your imagination. You're worn out from seeing after the baby. It was nothing. Don't be upset."

But Mrs. Barfoot was not comforted by his reassurances. She knew what she had seen. And so did Era Mae and Mrs. Cone. When Mrs. Barfoot was calmer, they listened to her description of the tall, dark-haired man, and they said softly, "Yes. We know. We have seen him, too."

Then the whole pent-up story of the ghostly visitations came pouring out, the fears, the apprehensions, the unanswered questions.

"Who is he?" they asked repeatedly. "Who is he? And why is he here?"

"I don't know who is is—all I know is that I am not going to stay here. I want to move. Now!" Mrs. Barfoot declared.

And they did. The Barfoot family moved from their rented house at 122 Orion Street in Troy to a farmhouse out in the country.

Before they left, Mrs. Barfoot asked some of their neighbors, people who had lived in the neighborhood a long time, about the history of the house, asked if any strange things had ever happened there.

"You mean you've finally seen the ghost?" one of the neighbors

After the accounts of the ghostly visitations came pouring out, the Barfoot family moved from their rented house at 122 Orion Street (above) in Troy to a farmhouse in the country.

asked. "We wondered why you had never asked about it. Everybody knows your house has been haunted for a long time. That's the ghost of a murderer—at least he was tried and convicted and hanged for murder—in that house. His name was Tom Johnson. You've heard about him, haven't you? There is even a song about him."

So from conversations with neighbors and from reading yellowed newspaper clippings, the Barfoot family pieced together the story of their ghost, the story of Thomas Johnson.

Tom Johnson, they learned was one of three men hanged in Troy on a bright March day in 1899. He and two accomplices, Richard Hale and Sam Rivers, were given death sentences for the murders of Mrs. R. A. Myers and her widowed daughter-in-law, Mrs. Ida Myers.

The elder Mrs. Myers, they heard, had continued to live at the family home in rural Pike County after the death of her husband. She was the mother of fifteen children, some of whom lived nearby. In addition to running a three-horse farm, she operated a small store near her house.

In late 1898, Mrs. Myers' daughter-in-law, Ida, was living with her, occupying a bedroom across the wide hall from the bedroom where the elder Mrs. Myers slept. The two widows were congenial, were company for each other.

John Cook, the twenty-three-year-old hired man, slept in a shed room at the back of the house.

Neighbors, including Mrs. Myers' son John, were awakened before dawn on December 17, 1898, by a brilliant glow in the dark sky and by the insistent clanging of a big farm bell.

"It's Old Lady Myers' house!" they exclaimed. And they hurried to the scene.

Dan Cowart and the Forehand boys were the first to arrive. They found Mrs. Ida Myers lying in the yard near the blazing house. She appeared to be dead. Mrs. Rachel Ann Myers, mortally wounded by blows from an ax, was begging someone to help her put on her clothes. John Cook, bloody from wounds on his head, was wandering around the yard in a dazed condition. It was Cook, testimony at the trial revealed, who rescued the two women from the burning house and who rang the bell to summon help.

John Myers, when he arrived a few minutes later, hurried back home to get his wagon to move the victims to his house.

When Myers returned, Tom Johnson and Richard Hale had joined the growing crowd in the yard, and they helped put the two women and Cook on a mattress in the wagon bed. Johnson went with them to John Myers' house where he washed the blood from Cook's wounds and tried to make the young man comfortable. Mrs. Ida Myers was dead, and the family realized that Mrs. Rachel Ann Myers could not long survive the battering she had received.

Meanwhile, Richard Hale had volunteered to ride into Banks to send a telegram (there were no telephones in the area) to Sheriff Sam Reeves informing him of the vicious attacks on the occupants of the Myers' home and asking him to bring bloodhounds to the scene. Hale borrowed a horse from Coward and used Sol Vickers' saddle for the ride into Banks.

It was Tom Johnson who suggested sending for the bloodhounds, John Myers recalled. Johnson had been a constable in that beat and was familiar with procedures for dealing with crime.

It was also Johnson who unloaded a wash pot and an egg crate from his wagon and went into Louisville with George Johnson (no kin) to get a coffin for Mrs. Ida Myers. He had, years before, brought the coffin for her husband, Elijah Myers, and John Myers wanted a coffin just like it for her.

A few days later, Johnson brought a coffin for Mrs. Rachel Ann Myers. He helped put the corpse in the coffin, and he put the lid on. At the graveyard, it was Johnson who removed the lid from the coffin (presumably so that some of the mourners could take a final look at the deceased) and who put it securely back in place.

Johnson and Hale helped fill the graves after first "Miss Ida" and then "Miss Rachel Ann" were buried, and Johnson and Hale helped mound the dirt on the fresh graves.

The two men were as neighborly, as helpful, as concerned as two men could possibly be. On the day following the tragedy, a Sunday it

143

was, Johnson even found occasion to hand over to John Myers some money he owed Mrs. Rachel Ann Myers for eggs he had sold for her in Union Springs.

So the entire community was shocked several weeks later when Sheriff Sam Reeves arrested Tom Johnson and Richard Hale and charged them with the murders of the two women. Robbery, officers said, was the motive.

The arrests followed a lengthy confession from a Negro, Sam Rivers, whom the sheriff had taken into custody for questioning. The sheriff became suspicious of Rivers, it was said, when he learned that Rivers had paid for purchases at a store with gold coins. Gold coins had reportedly been stolen from the Myers' home the night of the murders.

During that questioning, Rivers confessed to being present when the Myers women were slain and the house set fire, and he named Johnson and Hale as the men responsible for the crimes. He was forced at gunpoint, he said, to accompany the two men to the house.

Rivers told of moving a bee gum beneath a rear window to gain entrance to the house, of hearing the sound of two heavy blows from the bed where Cook was sleeping, of seeing the older Mrs. Myers being struck with an ax when she came to investigate the disturbance in Cook's room, of hearing "Miss Ida" Myers plead for her life as she was being axed down, of the rifling of trunks in search of money, and, finally, of helping to pour kerosene on Cook's bed and on floors at other places in the house, of setting fire to the oil, and of fleeing the scene.

Johnson and Hale maintained their innocence, and Johnson's wife, his mother, and his nine-year-old son Charlie (he told of being awakened the night of the murders to try on a new suit his father had brought him from Union Springs) confirmed their alibis.

But the members of the jury believed the story Sam Rivers told. On February 24, 1899, Johnson, Hale, and Rivers were found guilty of the murder charges. The date for their hangings was set for March 31, 1899.

So the crowds gathered in Troy on that final day in March 1899,

144

coming by train, wagon, buggy, horseback, and on foot to watch the triple hangings. There was a somber feeling among the crowds, nothing of the carnival spirit that sometimes marked such events.

They talked in hushed tones of the farewell visit paid Johnson by his wife and mother, and they told of how Hale had been baptised in jail by the Reverend J. D. Hall, rector of St. Mark's Episcopal Church.

Spectators near the jail watched the procession leave the side entrance at 11:00 a.m. for the journey to the gallows. First came a detachment of the Troy Rifles followed by the prisoners in a carriage driven by J. S. Carroll (Hale had traded at Carroll's store for many years, and Carroll asked to be permitted, as a final courtesy to a good customer, to provide the condemned men a ride to the gallows in his carriage) with another group of the Troy Rifles behind the vehicle. Then came Sheriff Reeves and his staff, all on horseback, with a carriage filled with friends of the men behind the lawmen. The Reverend J. D. Hall's buggy completed the procession.

The gallows stood near the Troy City Cemetery, not far from the site of the house on Orion Street that Era Mae Barfoot and her family would occupy some thirty years later. The platform with its paraphernalia of death was enclosed by a plank fence, sixteen feet high, built without cracks large enough to peep through.

Prayers, hymns, and testimonials at the gallows marked the final moments of life for the three men. Somehow the scene almost took on the feeling of a revival meeting.

Sam Rivers was the first to mount the platform. He spoke for almost half an hour, proclaiming that God knew he had told the truth about the murders of the two women.

After Rivers was pronounced dead and his body was removed, Hale and Johnson mounted the stand together. Both men declared they were innocent. Hale (he wore a bunch of fresh violets on the lapel of his coat) warned the young men in the crowd of the danger of keeping bad company, and Johnson promised his friends to meet them in heaven.

Several of the Myers men, sons of the murdered woman, shook

145

hands with Hale and Johnson and wished them well. One of the men prayed for the souls of Johnson and Hale "in a better world."

Then it was over...

It has been a long time since the ghost of Tom Johnson, if indeed that is who it was, stalked the home of Era Mae Barfoot, but she has never forgotten the sounds associated with his appearances nor has she ever forgotten those burning, penetrating eyes.

Every now and then she plays and sings snatches of a folksong written about those hangings,

> Johnson said to the sheriff,
> "Paint my gallows red, paint my gallows red."
> Johnson said to the sheriff,
> "Paint my gallows red
> So the whole Myers family
> Will know I'm dead."

There are other stanzas of the song, but the one about Johnson and the red gallows is sung the most often.

And as she plays and sings, she still wonders—why did Tom Johnson's restless spirit come to their home? Was there something about her grandmother that reminded him of the elder Mrs. Myers? Did he come to prove that he would do the old woman no harm? Had someone closely connected with the murders occupied the house before the Barfoot family moved in? Did Tom Johnson have memories that pulled him back to the house on Orion Street?

Why did he come? Why?

146

One evening Nikki Davis, a photographer for an Alabama newspaper, was visiting the Selma, Alabama, home of Kathryn Tucker
Windham. From a small Mississippi farming community, Nikki
(above, left) has always had a reputation for integrity and honesty.
She decided to make photographs in Kathryn's house—and two
rolls of film were shot that evening. The next day Nikki was developing them casually at her newspaper office when, "Suddenly I
almost overturned the developing tank," she explains. One of the
negatives she was developing showed a ghost! Nikki learned later
that she had discovered Jeffrey (above, right), destined to become
the most widely known ghost that has ever "lived" in the South.

Afterword to the Commemorative Edition

In the mid-1960s—maybe because she had publishing friends in north Alabama, or maybe because she thought it would sell and she sure could use the money, or maybe just because she wanted to see if she was up to the challenge—Mother decided she would write a cookbook. *Treasured Alabama Recipes* became an instant big seller, largely because of the stories that accompanied the family collection of recipes.

Shortly after the release of the cookbook, Margaret Gillis Figh, one of Mother's college English professors, called her. "Kathryn, you are going to write another book, and this time it doesn't need to have any recipes in it. It needs to be a book of stories," Dr. Figh told her. "I'll be your collaborator if you like."

About this same time unexplained occurrences began in our house.

I was the only child still at home, my older sister and brother by then off at college. One afternoon Mother and I were in the kitchen rolling out cookie dough. Our house was small but big enough. The narrow kitchen immediately adjoined the small dining room, which opened through paned double doors into the living room.

That afternoon is indelibly imprinted in my memory. I'd floured the rolling pin and Mother had dampened the counter so the edges of the waxed paper wouldn't roll up. We'd sprinkled more flour on the waxed paper—when making cookies nothing should stick to anything else—and the lump of dough was plopped down and ready to roll out.

At that very moment we heard a ruckus in the living room unlike anything I've ever heard since: loud and scratching noises that seemed to come from not one particular area of the room, but rather from a room filled completely with the unsettling sound as though the midget demons of hell might have been turned loose all at once.

We looked at each other, startled, and moved to investigate. Mother wiped flour on her apron as she hurried to open the double doors into the living room. At the first movement of the doors the room became totally silent—no, eerily silent. I was right beside my mother, looking through the panes into the room. "What was that, Mama?" I asked her more out of curiosity than fear. She hesitated. "I have no earthly idea," she said finally.

We stood there for a minute before Mother dismissed it as a squirrel that might have fallen down into the fireplace, though there was no squirrel. There was nothing in that room except the furniture. We went back into the kitchen. As soon as the dough was almost thin enough to make acceptably crisp cookies, it began again, this time louder and with more force than before. And again, the minute Mother pushed the door, it all stopped. Not one item in the room was disturbed. Not one picture was crooked. Not one glass paperweight had fallen from the mantel.

Though Mother and I waited with some anticipation, the remainder of that day was quiet, ordinary. But in the weeks and months that followed, the unaccountable goings-on continued. They began with loud footsteps clumping down the hall, the steps ending abruptly just inside my brother's bedroom with a jarring slam of the door.

Subsequent strangeness took the form of furniture rearranging, not just shifting a bit as it would if a foundation was settling, but honest-to-goodness interior redecorating—beds rearranged to balance dressers moved from one wall to another. Freshly baked cakes flying—not falling, but *sailing*—off the dining room table. We were amazed, entertained, puzzled, but we were never frightened. My brother and sister pooh-poo-hed our stories on their first visits home from college. But as the unusual goings-on manifested themselves to my siblings, they, too, were intrigued.

DILCY WINDHAM HILLEY

⌒

My mother was a multifaceted woman.

She taught a Sunday school class and made sure we went to church twice on the Sabbath. She was a believer.

She also was generous, perhaps to a fault. One Christmas we got extra stockings. As always, we drove down later to my grandmother's house in Thomasville, but Mother made an un-expected detour down a dirt road that she chose at random. We saw an African American woman walking with two small children. They were total strangers to us.

Mother stopped the car and asked me to give the children our extra stockings that were filled with candy, toys, and fruit. The children's mother's eyes sparkled.

"Santa Claus has come for you at the store and now he's come here," she told the children.

That was so like Mother. She told me about visiting a poor family with her father, who was a country banker, when she was young. She played in the dirt with the family's children that afternoon, and later she and her father shared in their mea-ger evening meal.

"You're not better than they are," her father told her when they left. "You're just used to better things." She remembered the lesson all her life.

On the other hand, she believed in the supernatural.

I was skeptical of Jeffrey and her stories. Whenever some-one asked me if I believed, my stock reply was, "Sure! Jeffrey sent me to college."

That always drew a laugh from the visitor and a wry smile from Mother.

One day, I was preparing to leave Selma for a job in New Mexico. My suitcase was packed and on my bed. Knowing that I had a long way to drive and that it would be many months before I saw Mother again, I embraced her in a lengthy good-bye hug.

Suddenly, my suitcase jumped from my bed, flipped over twice in the air, and landed beside me.

Mother and I just stared at each other.

"Jeffrey," she finally whispered. She wore the same wry smile.

I hit the road quickly. After that, I, too, was a believer.

BEN WINDHAM